Nicky Fifth

For Hire

by Lisa Funari Willever

Franklin Mason Press
Trenton, New Jersey

For Baby Timothy Todd

Franklin Mason Press is proud to donate twenty-five cents from the sale of each Nicky Fifth chapter book to the Sunshine Foundation. For more information about their work, turn to page 161.

Franklin Mason Press ISBN: 978-0-9760469-3-6
Library of Congress Control Number: 2007905883

Text Copyright © 2007 Lisa Funari Willever
Cover Photography © 2007 Paula Funari
www.paulafunariphotography.com
Cover Design by Peri Poloni-gabriel
www.knockoutbooks.com

Editorial Staff: Marcia Jacobs, Brooks Spencer, Linda Funari

The Nicky Fifth Series

Book 1
32 Dandelion Court
2007-2008 New Jersey Battle of the Books Selection

Book 2
Garden State Adventure
2005-2006 New Jersey Battle of the Books Selection

Book 3
For Hire

Contents

Chapter One

Details, My Friend, Details

Being the oldest kid in any family has its good and bad points. Being the oldest kid in my family was suddenly becoming a full-time job. When I turned twelve, I was sure that it would all be good; more freedom, less rules. I should have known better. Sure, I had more freedom, but there was something I hadn't quite counted on - more responsibilities. Without realizing it, I became a mini-adult and it happened so fast, I didn't even see it coming.

One day, I was just one of the kids, goofing around and getting in trouble. The next day, I was supposed to be setting an example and I should always know better. Instead of watching television in the morning, I was tying shoes and cutting waffles. Instead of making lists of things that I wanted, my mom was leaving hints that their anniversary was coming. When you're eight or nine, growing up seems so cool. Now, I found myself looking at my brother and sisters and thinking they were pretty lucky.

We were a few weeks from the beginning of a new school year and no one was more excited than my mom. She was about to start teaching kinder-garten in a new district and she was probably more excited than her students. Actually, given the stories of her students screaming, kicking and crying on the first day of school, I'm sure she was more excited.

Like clockwork, every August it was the same story. My mom would open the Sunday newspaper and look at the ads for Back-to-School sales. She circled what she needed and what she thought we needed. She made dozens of lists, compared everyone's prices and then we went on shopping expeditions. We couldn't just go to one or two stores, we went to one or two dozen.

Of course, for a kid, no store on earth is quite as depressing as the teacher supply store. Unless you're related to a teacher, you'll probably never step inside one. If you do, it's one of the scariest places in the world. It's wall-to-wall bulletin boards, workbooks, notes to parents and grade books in every color. They have a section they call 'games' but every single 'game' teaches you something like multiplication, telling time, or manners. While I dreaded our trips to the teacher store, the smell of school supplies had the same effect on my mom as fruits and vegetables had on my dad. This was the one place where he couldn't control her spending because she couldn't even control it.

As my mom examined her new kindergarten gear, I realized that summer was almost over. While it wasn't the summer I imagined, it turned out pretty decent. Actually, since moving from my friends on Fifth Street in Philadelphia, I realized few things turn out how I imagine them. I also realized that the difference wasn't always bad. Our Garden State Adventure, consisting of seven New Jersey day trips, wasn't exactly the Magic Kingdom, but it was an experience. The most memorable moment, besides my best friend T-Bone driving my father crazy, was when the Governor's Office called and asked us to be unofficial Junior Ambassadors for New Jersey.

Our job was to visit different places in New Jersey and give reports on the state website. They told us we could begin now or wait until school started. I still wasn't sure what *unofficial* actually meant, but I was pretty sure that it meant working for free. We decided to enjoy the summer and wait until school started.

With the first bell getting closer, I decided not to waste a minute of what was left of the summer. I called T-Bone to see what he was doing.

"Hey, T-Bone, it's Nicky. What's up?"

"Not much," he answered. "Did you get a new pencil case?"

"Very funny," I laughed. What's going on?"

"My brother just got a job at the mall," he said.

"Which brother," I wondered, since T-Bone was the youngest of four brothers.

"Teddy."

"Really?" I asked, kind of shocked. Teddy was 17 years old and I never saw him without head-phones. In the year I've known T-Bone I don't remember hearing him speak, other than the occasional grunt. His whole life was music and he owned more CD's than a small music store. "Is he working at Music Mania?"

"No."

"Turbo Tunes?"

"No."

"Those are the only two music stores at the mall. Isn't he working in a music store?" I asked.

"No," T-Bone answered, "they weren't hiring, so he's selling shoes."

"Shoes? Your brother Teddy is selling shoes? Does he realize he'll have to talk to people?"

"Probably not," T-Bone laughed.

"Hey, maybe he can get us a discount."

"Not if you're foot is bigger than a size three."

"Size three?" I asked, confused.

"Yeah, well, he's working at Wiggle Worm."

"Wiggle worm?" I laughed. "Does he know

Wiggle Worm is for little kids?"

"Probably not, but who cares? At least he'll be making some money," T-Bone moaned. "I'd give anything to have a job."

"Tell me about it. My parents' 15th anniversary is in September and my mom leaves me hints everyday."

"Why is she telling you?" T-Bone wondered.

"I don't know," I admitted. "I guess when your twelve you have to start giving gifts."

"Hold on," T-Bone exclaimed, "if that's true, my brothers owe me some gifts!"

"Yeah, try and collect," I laughed.

"Good point," he shrugged. "So what are you getting your parents?"

"That's the problem," I explained. "I only have $28.00 in the blue sock in my sock drawer. Maybe I ought to get a job at Wiggle Worm."

"That's not a bad idea," T-Bone nodded.

"What are you talking about?" I asked. "I was joking."

"No, that's really not a bad idea," he repeated.

"Except," I explained, "that it's illegal to hire

a 12 year old."

"Details, my friend, details," he said in a phony Jamaican accent.

"Details," I laughed, "is that all?"

"No, seriously, why didn't we think of this before? Let's get after school jobs."

"That sounds good," I sarcastically agreed, "I'll call the president of Nike and see if he has any positions for us."

"You know the president of Nike?" he asked.

I hung up.

Twenty minutes later, I heard the doorbell. A few seconds later, T-Bone came barreling into the kitchen with a thick newspaper under his arm. With his trademark stupid grin, he plopped the paper on the table. Oh, no, I thought.

"Fifth, take a look at this," he said holding up the classified ads. "There's like a thousand jobs right here and I bet a lot of them would hire us."

"First of all, moron, I doubt any of them will hire us. You can't even get working papers until you're sixteen."

"Maybe they have a kids section."

"Yeah, they do," I shot back, "it's called the comics."

"I'm serious," he said, "if Wiggle Worm can hire my brother, we should be able to get jobs easy."

Before I could answer, I heard two very light, very fast feet heading in my direction. "I want a fruit snack," my three year old sister, Emma interrupted. "Mommy said you have to get it. I want a fruit snack. Mommy said you have to get it."

"Alright already," I said, "hold on."

"Hold onto what?" she asked.

"Your horses," said T-Bone, trying to help.

"What horses?" asked Emma. "I don't got no horses."

"You should've seen that one coming," I told him.

As I opened Emma's snack something occurred to me. If T-Bone could find us jobs that didn't involve little kids, but did involve getting paid, I was in. I was definitely in. "Where do we start?" I asked.

Chapter Two

Red Marks The Job

Before we started searching the want ads, T-Bone insisted that I find a red marker. He said he had seen his brothers do this a hundred times and they always circle the good jobs with a red marker. I dove into my mom's shopping bags and found blue pens, black pens, green highlighters, and 186 different color crayons. It was hard to believe she forgot something. Unable to find a red marker, I returned with a red crayon.

"What's that?" T-Bone asked.

"What do you think it is?"

"I know it's a red crayon," he said, "but we need a red marker."

"Who cares how we circle the jobs?"

"I don't know why," he answered with growing agitation. "I just know that every time I see my brothers looking for a job, they use a red marker and they always end up with cool jobs."

"Cool jobs?" I laughed, "One brother moves furniture all day, one answers the Pizza House phone, and one works at Wiggle Worm. Yeah, that red pen is pure gold."

"You don't get it Fifth. They're making money. It doesn't matter how much you like a job or what they pay you. The thing that matters is that they pay you."

We opened up the want ads and started at the top.

"Accountant, accountant, accountant, accountant," T-Bone read aloud as he moved his finger down the column. "I can't believe they only have accountant jobs."

"Hey, moron, they're in alphabetical order," I said, shaking my head.

"Oh, good," he said, "I thought I'd have to become an accountant."

"You? An accountant?" my dad laughed as he walked into the kitchen. "Just out of curiosity, why are you two coloring the newspaper?"

"We're looking for jobs," announced T-Bone.

His announcement must have been too much for my dad. Luckily he was standing in front of the sink when the orange juice he was drinking shot out of his nose. "You're looking for a what?" he asked, trying to keep a straight face, while wiping it up with a napkin."

"A job, Mr. A. Like working for a living or bringing home the bacon."

"T-Bone, you couldn't bring home bacon if you tripped over a pig with a death wish. Anyway, don't you think you're a little young to be pounding the pavement?"

"Oh, we're not gonna work for a concrete company. At least I don't think we are. We didn't get to the C's yet."

My dad didn't even bother trying to explain what pounding the pavement meant. "Good luck with that," he said, still laughing, as he walked out.

"Barber, bartender, brick and block layer," he read slowly and then looked up.

"What?" I asked.

"Do you want me to circle any?"

"I don't know, why don't you let me cut your hair and if it works out, I'll apply for the barber job."

"Ooo-kay," he said, "moving right along. Cake decorator, carpet installer, cashier, construction, data entry, deli-help."

"Keep going."

"You can cut my hair, Nick," my brother Timmy offered.

"What?" I asked, not even noticing that my brother, who has made a career of being my shadow, had walked into the room.

"You can practice being a barber on me," he replied.

"Why would you let him cut your hair?" asked T-Bone.

"Because he's gonna be a barber," Timmy answered matter-of-factly. We shook our heads and got back to the mission.

"Driver, hairdresser, machine operator, mechanic, painter, print shop, school bus driver, tree service, waitress. Anything grabbing you?"

"Sure, put me down for school bus driver.

I'm going there anyway."

T-Bone didn't laugh or even send a zinger back to me, he just kind of sat there. I couldn't believe it. He looked a little depressed and I almost felt sorry for him.

"Good morning, boys," my mom said as she came into the kitchen. "What's this? Your father tells me you're looking for jobs?"

"We were," said a downtrodden T-Bone.

"What's the problem? I think it's a great idea."

"You do?" I asked, expecting her to naturally side with my dad.

"Of course I do. Having a job teaches you responsibility and discipline, not to mention the value of a dollar. I've worked since I was 10 years old."

"Where did you work when you were only ten years old?" T-Bone asked. "Were you part of a circus family?"

"No, Tommy, I wasn't part of a circus. My aunt had a little gift shop and I worked there on weekends and all summer long. I learned so much at that store."

"Does she need anyone else?" asked T-Bone.

"Sorry, she retired fifteen years ago."

"Then I guess we're back to square one since we can't do any of these jobs," T-Bone said as he pointed to the newspaper.

"Hold on," said my mom. "You aren't looking for a job in the want ads, are you?"

"Yeah," I answered slowly, "Where else would we look?"

"You'll never find jobs for boys your age in the newspaper," she said as she grabbed a pad and a *red marker* from the junk drawer. As soon as T-Bone saw the red marker I could feel him staring at me, just waiting for me to make eye contact so he could say I told you so. I didn't look.

My mom pulled up a chair and sat down to walk us through the underage job market.

"You see, working is great, even for kids. Actually, it's great especially for kids. But a long time ago, people took advantage and ran sweat shops where they hired kids to make clothes."

"Do they have any sweat shops around here?" T-Bone interrupted. "I'm sure I could learn to make clothes."

"As I was saying," my mom continued, "the

owners of these factories took advantage of all of the workers, especially the kids. They made them work really, really long hours with no breaks and they paid them pennies. They also didn't make the factories safe and a lot of people died. So they made laws to protect children."

"Really?" asked T-Bone.

"Really. But I think they go a little over-board, making kids wait so long to work. I say if a kid wants to know the feeling of earning a dollar, they should be able to work. This country was built upon a work ethic. In fact, that's the problem with kids now days, too much recreation and too many video games. If you boys want to work, you should be able to work. I'll help you find jobs."

As she was speaking, her voice became more intense and as she got to the middle of what turned into her speech, I was waiting for someone to start playing God Bless America in the background.

"Cool," T-Bone shouted, throwing my mom a high five. She just waved.

"Just one more thing," I asked, "how will we find jobs?"

"You just have to know where to look. At your age, you can start by getting odd jobs."

"Finally, something you're qualified to do," I said to T-Bone.

"Very funny," he replied. "What's an odd job?"

"Basically, they're jobs that people don't want to do. Like mowing the grass, raking leaves, shoveling snow, dog walking, babysitting," my mom gushed.

"Okay," I said. "Say we wanted to do odd jobs, how do we find them?"

"There are plenty of things you can do. You can make flyers and give them to everyone in the neighborhood, put signs up in stores, things like that."

"Do you really think people will call?" T-Bone asked.

"It's worth a shot. Why don't you think of jobs you'd like to do and I can help you design a flyer. In the meantime, can you keep an eye on the kids while I go get this stuff organized?"

T-Bone seemed really happy, but I had second thoughts. This job thing could be a slippery slope and the end of carefree childhood as I liked it. I'd learned from experience that the more you do, the more they want you to do. If I wasn't careful, before I knew it I'd be paying bills, doing laundry, and cooking dinner. I had an uneasy feeling and I was starting to sweat. Just as I was about to back out, I realized it was too late. My mom and T-Bone had set the wheels in motion and there was no turning back. Before I knew it, I was Nicky Fifth for hire.

Chapter Three

Tommy Who?

While I watched Timmy, Maggie, and Emma, T-Bone spent the rest of the day thinking. He thought so hard that I had to wake him up twice. We decided that our best chance of getting hired would be to list as many jobs as possible. Besides my mom's ideas, we added shopper, errand runner, and pool cleaner. Neither one of us had any experience cleaning pools, but we figured it made us look better.

"We need a name for our company," said T-Bone.

"Our what?" I asked as Maggie put a floppy hat on my head.

"Our company," he replied. "If we're gonna do this right, we need a catchy name. How about T-Bone, Incorporated?"

"No." I said, drinking my pretend tea.

"Nicky Fifth, Incorporated?"

"Again, I'm gonna have to go with no."

"Acme Odd Jobs?" he suggested.

"Not unless you plan to move to the desert and hire a roadrunner."

"Then you'll have to come up with the name. I gave you my best ideas."

"If they're your best ideas, I don't know if I want you in my company," I said tossing a balled-up piece of paper at his head.

"Very funny," T-Bone answered, confident that I was kidding.

We sat in silence for a few minutes when Maggie walked back in with a towel draped over her arm. "Maggie, at your service," she announced.

T-Bone sat up and a smile wrapped around his big melon head. He grabbed my mom's pad and wrote it down. "I like it, I really like it," he said.

"You like what?" I asked.

"I like our new company name."

"What new company name?"

"At Your Service," he declared.

After a moment, I realized it wasn't bad.

"Okay, we have a name and a list of jobs we can do, so now we need to figure out how much to charge."

"That's a tough one," I said, shaking my head.

"Why?" T-Bone wondered.

"Because we don't know how much people get for any of these jobs. We don't want to work too cheap, but if we charge too much, no one will hire us."

"Good point," said T-Bone. "Let's negotiate with every customer."

At first, it sounded like a good idea, but after thinking about it I knew negotiating was the answer.

"Why not?" he asked.

"Because," I began, "We'll have to remember what we charge every person. We can't charge one person $10.00 to rake the leaves and someone else $15.00."

"Why not?" he asked.

"Because it's not fair. Plus, what if two customers know each other and they start talking about us? If some people found out they were paying more than other people, we could lose a lot of customers."

"Then what should we do?"

"What if we charge by the hour?" I suggested. "Everyone gets charged the same rate and it would be fair."

We thought we had covered everything; a name for our company, a list of services, and how we would charge people. We were both pretty happy until I realized we forgot something very important; we had no idea how much our hourly rate would be.

"I have an idea," said T-Bone. "I'll call my brothers."

I handed T-Bone the cordless phone and he began to dial his house. I found it doubtful that any of his brothers, especially Teddy, would give him a straight answer so I turned on the speakerphone. At the very least this would be an interesting conversation.

"Yeah," said a voice from T-Bone's house.

"Hello, Teddy?"

"Who is this?"

"It's me," answered T-Bone.

"Me who?" Teddy asked, even though he knew who it was.

"It's Tommy, your brother."

"Tommy who?"

"Your brother, Tommy," explained T-Bone.

"Tommy Rizzo?"

"Yeah, yeah, Tommy Rizzo."

"What do you want?"

"I have a question."

"Yes, you smell," said Teddy. "Next question."

"That wasn't even my question," T-Bone protested. "Now here's the question. If you were gonna do odd jobs, how much would you charge an hour?"

"Who's doing odd jobs?"

"I am," said T-Bone.

"You?" he laughed.

"Yeah, me," T-Bone answered.

"Who's gonna hire you?"

"I don't know. But if someone did, what

should I charge them?"

"It all depends. What kind of jobs are we talking about?"

"I don't know, like cutting grass or raking leaves."

"You can't even cut your own food. Who's gonna hire you to cut their grass?"

"I'm serious, Teddy. Wiggle Worm gave *you* a job, didn't they? Just answer the question."

"Well, if you want to know what I would charge my customers, I'll tell you. I wouldn't go a penny under $40.00 an hour."

"Really?"

"Absolutely," he said, not even trying to sound convincing.

"Okay, thanks," T-Bone said, hanging up. "He said to charge $40.00 an hour."

Suddenly, being the oldest kid in my family wasn't bad. I was so used to little kids annoying me that I never thought about how frustrating it would be to have everyone treat me like a baby. In a way, T-Bone was lucky. He was so dense; he couldn't even tell when people were messing with him.

"You know he's joking, right?" I asked.

"What do you mean?"

"I mean he's not serious."

"You think?"

"Yeah, I'm pretty sure," I said, rolling my eyes. "I think minimum wage is like $5.00 an hour and the Mayor probably doesn't make $40.00 an hour."

"Oh," he said, sounding disappointed.

"You really believed him?" I asked.

"No, no," he lied, "I knew all along."

Wow, I thought. It was like his brothers had cast a stupid spell over him. For a moment, I started to think about the power I could wield over my own brother and sisters. Then I got back to the task at hand. We needed to decide what our prices would be and I realized I would have to make a decision without T-Bone's help.

"Let's do $5.00 an hour," I suggested, tossing out the first number that came to mind.

"For real?" he asked, not sure if I was being straight with him.

"Yeah, for real," I answered.

Chapter Four

The Shoe

When my mom finished whatever it was she was organizing, T-Bone and I were still waiting for her to design our flyer. We made a list of all of the places we would pass them out. We decided to put them in the neighbors' mailboxes, on the bulletin boards at the stores, and at the library.

Before she could help us, my mom had to run an errand and my dad took the other kids for a ride. When my mom returned, she was carrying more bags from the teacher store. *What a surprise!* Lucky for her, my dad was still out with the other kids and I was the only one who saw her hide the stash.

"Hey, boys," she said as she lifted her sunglasses on top of her head. "How's the job hunt?"

"Actually, pretty good," I replied. "We're ready for you to make the flyers."

"Did you make of a list of jobs that you'd like to do?"

"Check," said T-Bone.

"Did you figure out how much you want to charge?"

"Check. And not only that, we found a name for our company."

"Your what?" asked my mom.

"Our company," T-Bone repeated.

"Oh," she said, slightly shocked. "I didn't realize you boys were this serious. Let's go make that flyer."

When my mom was finished, the flyer looked great. It almost looked too good. It made it seem like we really knew what we were doing. I wondered how many people would call us and how much money we would make. I figured it would start slow and decided not to start spending the money in my head. Apparently, T-Bone was more confident and already making a list of things he would do with his half of the profits.

"I'll tell you one thing," he said. "As soon as I have enough money, I'm buying a snowboard."

"A snowboard?"

"Yeah, dude, a snowboard!" he exclaimed.

"Dude?" I asked.

"That's what you say if you're a surfer, skate-boarder, or snowboarder," he explained.

"Except," I reminded him, "that you're none of the above, dude."

"Not for long," he said, throwing his hands back behind his head.

"Quick question," I began, "even if we make enough money for you to buy a snowboard, then what?"

"What do you mean?"

"Well, I don't think you can snowboard on Petunia Lane or Dandelion Court."

"I'll go to Vermont."

I didn't want to ask, but I did. "How are you going to Vermont?"

"Details, my friend, details," he replied in his

fake Jamaican accent again.

Before I could question him about the details, the doorbell rang and rang and rang. On one ring, I usually walk to the door, on two rings I usually run, but on three or more rings, I ignore the whole thing. I learned a long time ago that no one, other than Emma or Maggie, keeps pushing the button.

I turned my head toward the front door and saw my dad walk in, followed by Emma, Timmy, and Maggie. He looked like a mother duck, followed by a row of ducklings.

"Where's your mother?" he asked.

"Working," T-Bone answered.

"Not you," said my dad, shaking his head and making a point to look at me.

"She's upstairs," I told him.

"Nicky, Nicky, Nicky, Nicky," said Maggie. "Look, look, look, look."

I turned around and Maggie was holding a new doll three inches from my nose.

"Look, Nicky, look, look. Daddy bought me a doll. Daddy bought me a doll."

"Great," I said, trying to duck.

"And daddy got Timmy a new baseball glove and Emma got a stuffed elephant."

I raised one eyebrow and looked at my dad. He was clearly avoiding my stare.

"And," I said, waiting to see what he bought for me. No answer. "And," I repeated.

"And Daddy forgot you," Maggie laughed, finishing my sentence.

"Don't be silly. Of course, we didn't forget Nicky," my dad said, reaching into a bag and pulling out a cardboard lemon air freshener. "Here you go, Nick."

"Are you kidding?" I asked. "That's from the car wash."

"No, it isn't," he said.

"Yes, it is," Maggie insisted. "That's the old one. They gave us a new strawberry one today."

"Trying to pass off an *old* air freshener as my gift?" I asked shaking my head.

"Alright, the air freshener isn't really a gift."

"No kidding," I smirked.

"But, I didn't forget you," he said, "I just didn't know what you would want."

"Nuh-uh," Maggie tattled. "When we were driving home, you said darn, I forgot to get Nicky something."

"Thanks, Mags," my dad said, taking a deep breath. "Sorry, Nick. We were in a hurry. I'll catch you next time."

"Don't worry about buying anything for Nick," said T-Bone. "Pretty soon he'll have enough money to buy whatever he wants."

"Oh, that's right," my dad teased, "I forgot that you guys are going to be accountants."

"No way, Mr. A., we changed our minds. We're going to be odd."

"If you can get paid for being odd, Tommy, you'll make your first million before you hit ninth grade."

"From your mouth to God's ears," T-Bone said, looking up.

"We're not gonna be odd," I explained, "we're gonna do odd jobs."

"What kind of odd jobs?" he asked.

Before we could answer, Maggie interrupted,

"Hey, where's my doll's shoe? I can't find my doll's shoe. Help me find my doll's shoe."

"I don't know," my dad said, pretending to look around the room. "I don't see it."

"You didn't look, daddy. You didn't look. Find my doll's shoe. Please, daddy."

"Honey, we'll find it later. So, Nick, what kind of odd jobs?"

Before I could answer, I heard the loudest banging, bumping, and screaming I had ever heard. It was awful and it was clear that someone was falling down the basement steps. My dad, who was standing near the door, turned, shrieked, and took that flight of stairs without touching a step. I looked from the top I and saw Emma, lying on her back, screaming.

"Mom, mom, help, help," Timmy ran off.

"Nicky, grab the phone and the flashlight, hurry," yelled my dad from the basement. "And get your mother!"

I grabbed the flashlight and the cordless phone and ran to the bottom of the steps. "Is she okay?" I asked, drowned out by her screaming and crying.

"I don't know," said my dad, shining a light at her eyes to check her pupils. "Nick, call the doctor. It's on the speed dial."

I dialed the doctor, handed the phone to my dad, and tried to calm Emma down. It was no use. She was screaming and couldn't hear a word I was saying. I heard foot steps and, expecting to see my mother, turned to get out of the way. Instead it was Maggie, holding her one-shoe doll.

"Did anyone find my doll's shoe yet?" she yelled with her hands on her waist.

"What," my dad screamed, about to lose his temper. "Can't you see your sister's hurt?"

"But I can't find her shoe," she persisted.

"Nicky, get her upstairs," my dad yelled as he simultaneously checked Emma's legs and listened to the automated directions from the doctor's office.

In a moment, my mom was by Emma's side, slightly less composed than my dad.

"Don't move her," my dad warned as my mom tried to pick her up. "She fell pretty hard."

My mom was trying to calm Emma down when Hurricane Maggie stomped down the steps.

"I'm still waiting for the shoe," she said. "Is anybody listening to me?"

"Get upstairs, now!" my dad hollered.

When she got to the top, I heard her ask T-Bone if he had seen the shoe.

While my dad was on hold, Emma stopped crying and seemed to go to sleep. I was pretty sure that wasn't good and from the look on my parents' faces, I knew I was right.

"Forget it," my dad yelled. "I'm not waiting. We're taking her to the hospital right now."

My mom ran for the van keys and like clock-work, Maggie appeared and demanded that someone help her find her doll's shoe. I tried to catch her, but it was too late. She was on a mission and completely oblivious to the fact that Emma could be really hurt.

Luckily, at this point, my dad wasn't listening to a word Maggie was saying. He told my mom to start the car and he gently picked Emma up and tucked her into her car seat. My mom sat next to her and the rest of us piled into the van. It wasn't until we got to the emergency room that we realized T-Bone had jumped in, too.

We pulled up and my mom ran in with her. My dad parked the car and just shook his head when he realized T-Bone was still with us. We only waited a few minutes before they said we could go in and see her. First, my dad went back with my mom and then he came out for the rest of us, including T-Bone.

Emma had just started to open her eyes when we walked into the room. My mom and dad were talking to her and holding her hand when Maggie pushed her way to the front. Without saying a word, she held up the one-shoe doll. As if he was suddenly remembering the whole doll episode, my dad grabbed the doll like he was going to tear the head off. Lucky for Maggie, my mother grabbed it and put it aside. She gave Maggie *the look*. Obviously, Maggie understood *the look,* because she went and sat in a chair and didn't mention the shoe again.

Just then a nurse came in and started examining Emma. She said that they didn't believe she had broken any bones but that the doctor wanted her to have a CAT scan.

"They don't have a cat," said T-Bone, trying to be helpful. Everyone just looked at him.

"As I was saying," the nurse continued. "She's coming around and may only have a slight concussion, but the CAT scan will let us know more."

They said we could all walk over to the imaging department and they even let Maggie and Emma ride in the wheelchair together. When we arrived, there was a huge window where you could watch the CAT scans. My mom held her and tried to explain that it wouldn't hurt and the machine would just take a picture of her brain. Emma never took her eyes off of it. As an old man emerged from the machine, Emma seemed really scared. I wondered if she thought it was like a time machine and that when the old man went in he was only five years old.

A technician came out of the office and called her name. As my mom started heading toward the door, Emma whispered in her ear, "Take me to Maggie."

"What?" my mom asked.

"Take me to Maggie," she repeated, as if she were uttering her last words.

Holding Emma, my mom walked over to the

wheelchair where Maggie was still sitting and stroking her doll's hair. Emma pointed for my mom to bend down. Just as Emma got close to Maggie's ear, we heard her say the five words we'll never forget, "Maggie…I have the shoe."

"I knew it," Maggie said, jumping up. "I knew it! I knew someone had the shoe. I told you so. See Dad, I told you so."

My mom and dad just looked at each other, ready to wring both of their necks but relieved that we didn't *really* need the CAT scan to know Emma was okay. After her test was completed the doctors told my parents something we always knew, Emma had a hard head. They said to keep an eye on her overnight and that she should be fine.

When we returned home, my mom told Emma she had to stay on the couch and propped her up with some pillows and blankets. She popped in a movie, but before she could turn around, Emma was already off of the couch.

"Honey, you need to stay on the couch and rest," my mom insisted.

"No, mommy, first I have to get something."

She walked into the kitchen, opened up the refrigerator, and grabbed the butter dish. She took off the lid and like magic, one cold, lightly buttered doll shoe appeared. By now, everyone was exhausted. At the time of the fall, my parents were pretty calm, at least my dad was, but now *what could have happened* was sinking in. I heard my parents talking about how Emma could have been seriously hurt and my mom suggested making her wear her bike helmet around the house.

Later, before I went to bed, I knocked on my mom's bedroom door.

"Come in," she said, sitting on the bed with a pile of bills and her checkbook. "What's up, Nick?"

"Mom, I was wondering," I began, "is there any way to delete something from our flyer?"

"Sure, what do you want me to take out?"

"Babysitting," I said, "definitely, babysitting."

Chapter Five

Thomas Speaking

The next morning, when I woke up, I saw a pile of papers on my dresser. I walked over to see what they were. My mother had left the flyers with a note saying she was out with the other kids. I figured she was at the teacher supply store again.

I grabbed the flyers and looked them over. They looked great so I called T-Bone to tell him they were ready. About five minutes later, the doorbell rang and I saw T-Bone's bike leaning on the front steps. I got my bike and we started delivering them. It was about 95 degrees and it took three hours. After we hung our last flyer at my dad's supermarket we went to the frozen food aisle. We stood over the frozen vegetable section pretending to check out the broccoli, but we were really trying to get cool. After five minutes, we heard a familiar voice.

"Nick?"

"Hey, dad," I said as I turned around.

"Frozen vegetables, Nick? Frozen vegetables?" he said, pretending to be disappointed. "Have I taught you nothing?"

"I know, I know, nothing in the world is better than fresh fruits and vegetables, blah, blah, blah, but you don't have a freezer in your department."

"So what are you two up to?" he asked.

"We passed out a hundred flyers," said T-Bone.

"Actually, we better get home so we don't miss any calls," I warned.

"Alright, sport. Good luck," said my dad as he went back to the paradise he calls the produce section.

We went right back to my house and waited by the phone. We put my phone number on the flyer because we didn't trust T-Bone's brothers to take messages for us. We grabbed the cordless phone and sat on the front steps. Thirty minutes went by and not one call. Then an hour passed, followed by two.

"Maybe we should pass out more flyers," T-Bone suggested.

"Maybe," I said, even though I was sure that wasn't the answer.

"Maybe we should have kept babysitter on there."

We thought about it for a moment, remembered Emma's fall, and decided that we made the right decision to delete it.

"I guess I won't be snowboarding in Vermont," said T-Bone.

"You don't know that," I said, trying to cheer him up.

"Fifth, it's been four hours and no one has called."

"Maybe we're not giving it enough time," I suggested.

"Maybe we should do like the furniture stores and have a giant going out of business sale."

"Go out of business already?" I asked.

"No, you don't have to actually go out of business, you just say you are."

"That sounds kind of sneaky."

"I guess," he said, "but we have to think of something quick."

"Definitely," I agreed.

For the rest of the night, the only time the phone rang was when T-Bone called to see if anyone else had called.

The next morning my mom knocked on my door. "Nick, are you awake?"

"No," I answered.

"Good," she said as she pulled up the shades. "Did you pass out all of your flyers yesterday?"

"Yeah," I said, hiding from the sunlight.

"Then why the long face?"

"Because it didn't work."

"What do you mean it didn't work?" she asked.

"We rushed right home and sat here all day. We waited and waited and no one called, not even a wrong number."

My mom started laughing. "Nicky, you only

gave out the flyers yesterday. What did you expect?"

"I expected people to start hiring us and they haven't."

"Honey, it's the end of the summer. People are on vacation and getting ready for school. I'm sure they're just really busy. I'll bet a lot of people got your flyer, read it, and put it on the refrigerator. Once things calm down, you'll get some calls. If you do a great job, those people will tell other people."

"How long will that take?"

"Nicky, it takes time to build a business, even an odd-job business. Just be patient and give it a few months to get started."

I called T-Bone and he answered his phone by saying, "At Your Service, Thomas speaking."

"T-Bone?" I asked, not expecting to hear what I had just heard.

"Hey, Nick," he said, "how do you like the way I answered the phone? Pretty professional, huh?"

"You do realize that no one has your phone number, right?"

"What do you mean?"

"I mean, Thomas, you don't have to say at your service when your phone rings. Any one who has a flyer is gonna call my house. They don't have your number."

"Oh, yeah," he said. "Do you want me to come over and answer the phone at your house?"

"No," I said. "Anyway, I talked to my mom today and she said that with the end of summer, vacations, and back-to-school, people are too busy right now. After the summer, we should start getting some calls."

"That's good, right?"

"Except that I'll never have enough money to get my parents an anniversary gift and my mom left more hints last night."

"Hey, I've got an idea for you," said T-Bone. "But first, will we be off today?"

I thought it was funny that, just because no one called, we were off. We hadn't even done one day's work yet and now we were off. "Yeah, we're off. Why?"

"I have an idea about how you can get a present for your mom and dad."

"Go ahead," I challenged.

"When my mom and I went to pick up my brother at the mall last week, we grabbed burgers at Wrangler Ray's."

"Thanks, but I don't think my parents want to have their anniversary dinner at Wrangler Rays."

"If you'd let me finish," he said with my trademark sarcasm. "They have this thing there. You collect points and pick prizes out of a catalog."

"How do you get points?"

"They have stickers on the cups. Small is 10 points, medium is 15 points, and large is 25 points."

"Yeah, but how many points do you need to get a decent prize? Is it like being at the arcade and needing four million points to get a back-scratcher?" I asked. "And where do I get the money to buy all those sodas?"

"Details, my friend, details."

Chapter Six

Details Inside

For several reasons, I didn't have too much faith in T-Bone's idea. I'm not sure if it was because he rarely leaves New Jersey, yet has a part-time Jamaican accent, or if it was just because he was T-Bone. The phone rang and it was him wanting to know if we were still off.

"You doing anything, right now?" he asked.

"I don't know. Why?"

"We could take the bus up to the mall and check out Wrangler Rays."

"I guess," I said. "Meet me at my house when you're ready and I'll check with my mom."

One good thing about where we moved was that it was close to everything. There was a bus stop near my street and the mall was only 5 minutes down the road. T-Bone came over and after bus fare and safety warnings from my mom, we were on our way. I thought we would head straight to Wrangler Ray's, but instead, we found ourselves standing in front of Wiggle Worm, laughing at T-Bone's brother, Teddy. He was in the middle of putting shoes on a little boy when the boy accidentally kicked him in the nose. While it would have been worth the trip just to watch Teddy work and bleed, we had our own work to do.

We took the escalator upstairs and walked over to Wrangler Ray's. There was a huge sign in the front window about the points system and the prizes.

"It says collect points and pick prizes. Details inside. Let's go," said T-Bone with uncharacteristic confidence.

We walked to the back of the line and waited our turn. I assumed we were buying sodas to start collecting the points, but T-Bone had other ideas.

"Thank you for coming to Wrangler Ray's. Can I take your order?" asked a teenage girl.

"Yeah, I'd like details," T-Bone said proudly.

"Excuse me," she said, raising her head.

"Details, my friend, details."

Oh, no, I thought, not the Jamaican accent. His insistence actually confused the girl so much that she called T-Bone's order on the microphone.

"One order of details," she said, scanning the cash register, unsure of what button to push.

Two seconds later a manager appeared and asked the girl what she had ordered. I wanted to stop her, but before I could open my mouth, she looked at her boss with a straight face and said, "I ordered details."

"Are you kidding me?" asked the manager. "We're in the middle of a rush and you're goofing around on the microphone?"

"Excuse me," I said, "it's not her fault. We came up to find out about the points thing and it says details inside. So my crazy friend asked for details. All we want are the rules."

The manager reached under the counter, tossed a catalog at us, and hollered into the microphone, "Next!"

"See," T-Bone said. "Piece of cake."

"Give me that," I said grabbing the catalog.

We found a half-empty bench outside and started to read about the program. I had to hand it to T-Bone, it looked like his idea could work. Collect points, stick them into a book, and turn them in for valuable prizes. All of the prizes probably required a lot of points, but T-Bone had an idea. There was no way we could drink that much soda. Actually, we could drink it, we just couldn't afford it. So, we decided to ask people if we could have their stickers. We read that it could take two weeks for prizes to arrive so we knew we had to get all of the points before school started. It sounded simple enough.

"Let's watch the operation," T-Bone suggested as if he were casing a house.

"The operation?" I asked.

"How should we ask people for their stickers?" he wondered. "I don't want to scare anyone."

"Just be polite and say, 'Excuse me, are you collecting the stickers?' If they say yes, say, 'Thanks, anyway,' if they say no, ask them if they would mind giving you their sticker."

As soon as I said it, the thought of actually approaching someone made the whole idea seem stupid. I also couldn't believe that I was giving him advice on how to beg people for stickers.

We sat outside the restaurant, watching person after person leave with their cups. The good news was that most people throw everything out except for their drink. They like to carry them around, afraid they may get thirsty and regret throwing them away.

Luckily, the sticker collecting books were hanging by the door and we didn't have to go back up to the register again. I grabbed a handful of books and decided to send T-Bone on the first mission. It was like one of those cool crime shows. I could be the profiler and scan the customers to see who he should approach. T-Bone could be the field guy who does the actual work. I figured it would take him months to catch on.

"Alright," I told him, "there's a man in a suit about to leave. I doubt he collects stickers. Go ask him."

Before he had time to think about it, T-Bone approached the gentleman.

"Excuse me, sir," he started.

"Yes?"

"Are you collecting the sticker from your soda?"

"Actually, my kids are," he said without even slowing down.

"Shot down," T-Bone said as he returned to the bench.

"That's alright he's only the first person. You'll get the next one."

T-Bone stopped and looked at me. I was sure he was about to send me out to get the next one, since we were doing it for my parents. Instead, he asked if he should do it with his hat on or off.

"On," I said. "Now, look, there's a lady with a double stroller. She can't have time to collect stickers. Try her."

T-Bone quietly walked back and stood near the frazzled mom. "Excuse me, ma'am. Are you collecting the stickers from the cups?"

"What stickers?" she asked.

"The ones on the cups," T-Bone said, pointing to the sticker on her cup.

"I don't know anything about it," she said. "What do you do?"

"Well, you collect the stickers from your soda cups and stick them in a book. When you get enough, you can get prizes."

"What kind of prizes?" she asked. By now she must have thought he worked for Wrangler Ray.

"Valuable ones," T-Bone answered

"Sure, I'll start collecting," she said. "Where do I get a book?"

"I'll get you some," he said with a smile.

He came back to the bench with a big grin on his face. "Hey, I just told that lady about the points."

"You know you don't work here, right?" I asked.

"Yeah, why?"

"Because you're supposed to be getting stickers, not recruiting people."

"Gotcha," he said.

I still thought the plan had potential, but a piece of cake, probably not. Without collecting one point, we decided to go home and come back early the next morning.

Chapter Seven

Calling Dibs

The next morning the phone rang early. It was T-Bone. "The mall opens at 9:30 today. I'll be over in a few minutes."

"T, I'm still sleeping. We don't have to open the mall and it doesn't take an hour to get there."

"Sorry, I just thought you wanted to get your parents a great gift. I looked through the catalog last night and you can earn trips, computers, even a car."

"Really?" I asked. "How great would it be if I could send them to an island or get them a new car?"

"I'm leaving now," T-Bone exclaimed.

"Alright, alright, I'm up."

I felt kind of stupid getting on the bus when I saw it was the same bus driver. I decided that it wouldn't be bad as long as she didn't know what we were doing. "Good morning boys," she said.

"Good morning," we answered.

"Going to the mall again?"

"Yeah, you'll be seeing us a lot until school starts," T-Bone announced.

"Really, why is that?" she asked.

"We're collecting points from Wrangler Ray cups," T-Bone stated as he took the seat behind the driver, "to get his mom and dad an anniversary present."

"That's some project."

"Yeah, we're all about the hard work," said T-Bone. "We actually own a company called At Your Service. We're still waiting for someone to hire us."

"What kind of work do you do?" she asked.

"Odd jobs," he answered proudly. "Here's our flyer in case you know of anyone who needs odd jobbers."

"Thanks," she said, clipping the flyer to her clipboard.

Luckily, before he could say another word, we were pulling into the mall.

"Good luck, boys," yelled the driver.

"Thanks," we yelled back, as we walked toward the entrance.

"Why did you have to tell her what we were doing?" I asked.

"Why not?"

"Because it's embarrassing and you don't even know where she lives."

"That's right," he said, sounding like my grandfather. "You never know."

Just as we approached the entrance doors, a man was unlocking them.

"Great," said T-Bone. "Could our timing be any more perfect? We shouldn't even have to share a bench with anyone."

When we got upstairs, much to our surprise, all of the benches were filled with old people.

"What, did they sleep here?" asked T-Bone.

"I don't know, but so much for perfect timing," I replied.

We walked over to yesterday's bench and

asked the woman if we could sit on the end. She asked us to repeat the question twice and then told us that she was saving it for her friend. We walked in Wrangler Ray's and there was a pretty decent crowd for the morning so we decided to just stand out front.

"Hey," I said, getting T-Bone's attention. "I think we screwed up."

"What do you mean?"

"I mean no one drinks soda this early."

"Wow," said T-Bone, talking a deep breath. "I never even thought of that. But wait, what about coffee and orange juice cups?"

"I'll walk around and check it out," I said.

The good news was that they did have stickers on the coffee and juice cups. The bad news was that almost everyone there had a refillable Wrangler cup. We had zero points and things were starting to look dim.

With no bench and no drinkers, we decided to take a walk around the mall. It was so quiet, it felt like we were breaking the law. We walked both levels and as we rounded the fountain, I saw something from the corner of my eye. Sticking out of the garbage can was the sticker end of a Wrangler Ray large soda.

"T-Bone, look over there," I pointed to a trash can and whispered.

"Don't move," he warned, as if he was sneaking up on a grizzly bear.

"I'll get the book open, you grab the sticker."

"Got it," said T-Bone.

He walked over, grabbed the cup, looked around, removed the sticker, looked around, and walked back. "Twenty-five points," he said, facing the other direction.

"Relax," I said, "we're not working for the C.I.A."

"Yeah, I know, but its fun pretending we are."

"Fine, I don't care what you do, just don't start talking into your shoe."

"Huh?" he asked.

"Your shoe, you know, like on the old spy show and the spy's shoe is really a phone? Never mind," I sighed.

I decided to let him do it his way, even if he insisted on pretending to be a spy. After all, we were spending all of the points on my parents. With one sticker and new enthusiasm, we returned upstairs. The mall was becoming more crowded with back-to-school shoppers and we scanned the area for an empty bench. I saw one directly across from the restaurant and we took a seat.

A moment later, an elderly man approached. "Excuse me," he said, "You're on my bench."

"Huh?" asked T-Bone.

"You're on my bench. I come here everyday and this is my bench."

"We saw it first," said T-Bone.

"I've been here since 8:00," he said, "I just went to the men's room."

"Yeah, but you didn't get anyone to save it."

"What?" he asked.

"If you leave your seat and you want to have it when you get back, you're supposed to make someone save it for you," T-Bone explained. "Everyone knows that."

"Listen, young man, I come here every day and sit on this bench. Why don't you go annoy someone else?"

"Did you call dibs?" T-Bone asked.

"What?" he snapped.

"I asked if you called dibs. If you had called dibs then you would get the whole bench."

"Is that a fact?" he asked as if he were up to something.

"Not only is it a fact," said T-Bone, "it's also true. Unless you want the front seat in a car, then you yell shotgun."

"Then lucky for me, I did call dibs," he said. "On May 27, 1999, I distinctly remember calling dibs."

T-Bone dropped his shoulders, sighed, and looked in my direction. "He distinctly remembers calling dibs. He wins."

I couldn't believe T-Bone was arguing with a little old man about a mall bench, or that he actually believed the man called 'dibs' in 1999.

"Listen," I said to the man, "we're sorry. We didn't know this bench meant so much to you. We'll move."

"Well, you might as well stay now," he mumbled. "Just stay on your half."

"Thanks," I said, holding out my hand. "I'm Nicky and this is my friend, T-Bone."

"And I'm Uncle Sam," he said, ignoring me.

"Nice to meet you, Sam," said T-Bone.

I rolled my eyes. Not only were we about to spend the day at the mall, begging people for stickers, now we had to share a bench with the grumpiest old man I had ever met. Trying to stay on our crowded half of the bench, T-Bone was practically sitting on top of me, while Uncle Sam was enjoying the comfort of his spacious half.

"So, how are you?" I asked, trying to make conversation.

"Listen, you can sit here, but there's a curtain between us," he said, pointing to an imaginary curtain. "If you keep bugging me, the curtain goes down. Got it?"

"Fine, whatever," I said.

T-Bone and I scanned the crowd. The quicker I could find someone for him to approach, the more room I would have.

"Look, two ladies are getting up."

"I'm on it," he said, walking like a junior spy.

He spoke to them, they smiled, and he ran back with a goofy smile, almost skipping. "What happened to your secret spy act?" I asked.

"Oh, yeah," he said, snapping back into spy mode. "But look, I got 50 points."

"Cool," I said, sticking them in the book.

"Hey, four ladies are getting up," he said, rushing back to the front.

We were finally on a roll. Soon, we had two pages of the book filled and I could barely keep up with him. It was amazing how easy begging came to him. I was sure it was because he was the youngest kid at his house. Watching T-Bone, I was beginning to understand why the old folks enjoyed people watching. I was supposed to be scoping the Wrangler Ray crowd, but it was so easy to get distracted.

I saw a lady with two little boys who refused to walk forward. As she begged them to turn around, they continued walking backwards and banging into people while she apologized. Another woman was trying to juggle shopping bags, her pocketbook, and a hot coffee. T-Bone spotted her, too, and looked like he was going to help her until he realized she wasn't holding a Wrangler

Ray cup. Uncle Sam stared at every person who walked by without any emotion until a teenager tripped and landed on his stomach.

Finally, a smile.

Chapter Eight

How Hard Could It Be?

By three o'clock, T-Bone had filled up one book and we were working on our second. I was starting to feel guilty about letting him do all of the hard work and decided to give begging a try. I saw an opportunity and approached an elderly couple. I felt like an idiot, but decided to try it anyway. How hard could it be? I wondered.

"Excuse me," I started, "Are you, uh, I mean, are you gonna, um, hi, I'm trying to find out if…"

"Oh, dear," said the woman, "what do you think he's trying to say?"

"I don't know," the old man replied, "are you okay, son?"

"Yeah, I'm just wondering if you, um, could let me, um, man this is really hard."

"I think I know what you're trying to say," the old man said, reaching into his pocket and taking out a quarter. "Here son, I hope this helps."

"Poor thing," said the woman.

The only thing more embarrassing than having people think I was an actual beggar was turning my head toward the bench and seeing Uncle Sam's sinister smile. I was hoping T-Bone didn't hear what had just happened, but it was too late.

"Good job, Fifth. Seventy-five more cents and you can get a burger."

"Very funny," I said, wanting to sit down, but determined not to be outdone by T-Bone. "That was my first one. I was just getting the kinks out."

I spotted a man in a suit and practiced my speech as I approached. "Excuse me," I said. "I'm trying to wonder if you like are trying to like cups and if you're sticky?" As it came out of my mouth, I knew it was very wrong. I hoped he didn't notice.

"Stay off of drugs, kid," he said, pushing past me. I guess he noticed.

I went back to the bench, humiliated and wondering how T-Bone could do it and I couldn't. Worse than that, I saw another big smile plastered on Uncle Sam's face.

"You ready to head back?" I asked.

"Hold on," he said, "two ladies in line are going to give me their points."

"How do you know?"

"They told me when I asked them."

I couldn't believe it. T-Bone was so good that people were promising him their points before they even ordered. A few minutes later, a woman came outside, handed T-Bone the points and two sodas. No way, I thought, they're even buying him sodas.

"Here you go," he said, handing me a large soda with a big grin. "Don't forget to take your sticker off!"

I just shook my head and we waited for the bus. As usual, the same bus driver picked us up.

"So, how did you boys make out?" she asked.

"Pretty good," said T-Bone, reading her name tag. "How's the route, Sandy?"

"A little slow today, but not too bad."

It's funny. You hang out with someone everyday and never know what their strengths are in the real world. With T-Bone, I never knew he was such a people person. It's like he could do no wrong and everyone loved him. It was becoming annoying.

"By the way, I'm T-Bone and this is Nicky."

"Well, it's nice to meet both of you."

"Nice to meet you," I said, nodding my head.

When I finally walked in my front door, I was exhausted. I wanted to go right to my room and sleep, but I stopped in the kitchen to see if anyone had called for odd jobs. My mom and dad were sitting at the table talking and Maggie was playing on the floor.

"How was your day, honey?" my mom asked.

"Fine."

"Were you guys at the mall this whole time?"

"Yeah."

"What do you do all day?" she asked.

"Maybe it's a girl," my dad teased.

"Nicky has a girlfriend, Nicky has a girlfriend," sang Maggie. Emma chimed in, too.

"I don't have a girlfriend. I was just hanging out," I hollered.

"Alright, alright," my dad raised his voice. "You don't have a girlfriend. Just keep it down."

"Did anyone call?" I asked my mom, my only true ally in the room.

"You mean like a girl?" she laughed. Traitor, I thought.

"No, I mean like a job."

"Sorry, honey, not yet."

As I climbed the stairs I heard Maggie singing the kissing song. I locked my bedroom door and took a nap. About an hour later someone knocked on my door. "Who is it?"

"Nick, Nick, it's me."

"Me who?" I asked, copying Teddy Rizzo.

"Timmy."

"Timmy who?"

"Timmy, your brother."

"Timmy Abruzzi?"

"Yeah, you know who it is."

"Alright, Timmy Abruzzi. What do you want?"

"I just want to ask you a question."

"Okay, well put it in writing and slip it under my door."

"Alright," he said, walking away.

Two minutes later a piece of paper shot under my door. I picked it up. Timmy wanted to hang out with me and T-Bone tomorrow. Ha, I thought to myself, no way. I plopped back on the bed and then it hit me. Timmy might have a knack for begging, too. God knows, he's had enough practice. I flew off the bed to catch him. Unfortunately, I opened my door and tripped right over him.

"So," I said, pulling myself up, "you want to hang out with us, tomorrow?"

"Yeah, Nick. I have my own money for the bus and everything."

"You'll have to get up early," I warned.

"I'll get up when you say. I promise."

"You know, you'll have to do whatever I say."

"Alright, Nick. I don't care. What do I do?"

"Well, it's kind of a secret, so you'll have to wait until we get to the mall." And just like that, another Wrangler Ray beggar was born.

Chapter Nine

Oh, Brother!

The next morning Timmy was up bright and early and I regretted not giving him a definite time to be ready. For two hours he knocked on my door every ten minutes. I wondered if bringing him along was a good idea after all.

We stood at the bus stop, this time with our new addition. Timmy stared at us, probably looking for some clue as to what we'd be doing. The bus arrived and we filed on, right to our usual seats.

"Good morning, T-Bone. Good morning, Nicky," said Sandy. "And who do we have here?"

"This is Nicky's brother, Timmy."

"Good morning, Timmy. It's nice to meet you."

"Hi," said Timmy.

When we arrived, Uncle Sam was already on our bench. I was convinced he lived at the mall and figured one day he would show up in his robe and fuzzy slippers. For obvious reasons, we decided that T-Bone would show Timmy how to beg for points. Sam had his usual I'm-a-grumpy-old-man-and-don't-talk-to-me face on, but the silence was weirder than usual.

"Good morning," I said, avoiding eye contact.

"Is it a good morning?" he asked.

"What?"

"Is it?" he repeated. "What makes it so good?"

Oh, brother, I thought. What makes one guy so miserable? Since I didn't have an answer for the good morning question, I ignored it. I watched T-Bone explain the system to Timmy and they were off. Within five minutes, they had 200 points. I hated to admit it, but they made a great team.

"Nick, Nick, look at all of these stickers!" exclaimed Timmy.

"Cool," I said, as I stuck them into the book, relieved that I wasn't out there begging.

"What are we doing with them?" he asked. "Do I get something?"

I hadn't counted on Timmy asking that question and I wasn't sure how to answer. If I told him we were getting a big gift for my parents, he would tell them. If I didn't tell him the truth, he would want something for himself. I quickly examined the situation and told him we were doing it to help old people. Satisfied, he ran right back to work.

"Ha!" I heard from the other end of the bench. "Doing it for old people? That's rich."

"It's a long story," I explained and Sam dropped the issue.

By lunch time, the sticker boys were on a roll and people loved them. T-Bone was pulling chairs out and delivering napkins. At one point, Timmy was pushing a stroller back and forth so a lady could take a few bites of her burger. They were dropping off stickers almost as fast as I could stick them in the book. T-Bone and Timmy came back to the bench when the lunch crowd slowed down. Suddenly, I had an idea.

"You know, I've been watching the people

when they leave and a lot of them are walking away with stickers still on their cups."

"Yeah, well, we can't get every single person, Nick," said T-Bone, out of breath and defending his work.

"I know. That's what I'm trying to say. A lot of people are walking around with their cups and throwing them out in other places."

"So you want to go to people's houses and ask if they have any cups?"

"No, stupid," I said. "Since its slow now, I want to check out the garbage cans around the mall."

"Oh," T-Bone nodded, as if he understood.

"So are you in?" I asked.

"Okay," T-Bone and Timmy said together.

I grabbed the books, looked at Uncle Sam, and just to be a wise-guy said, "Good day, Sir."

Sam just stared at us.

We slowly headed toward the other end of the mall, checking out the garbage cans along the way. At the middle of the mall, by the fountain, we saw some cups. They were right on the top and easy to grab. We peeled off the stickers and threw the cups back in the can. We were pretty excited, although I knew going from beggar to garbage picker wasn't exactly a step up.

"Nick, Nick, did you see that?" asked Timmy.

"See what?"

"That family over there just threw five cups away."

"Where?"

"Right there," he said, pointing to a garbage can.

We walked up to the can and couldn't see any cups. We looked a little closer and there they were, at the bottom. Unfortunately, the can must have just been emptied.

"T-Bone, see if you can reach them," I directed.

"Okay," he said. Luckily, he was so used to taking orders at home, he didn't even blink. He reached in and his hand disappeared. Soon, his arm, up to his shoulder had disappeared in the traditional mall-style garbage can with wide openings on the side.

"Can you feel anything?" I asked.

"No, but I know they're in here. My arm's just not long enough. You try."

"Who me?" I asked, almost insulted.

"Yes, your majesty," T-Bone shot back, definitely aware that I had been getting off pretty easy.

I reached in as far as I could and moved my hand around. I wasn't sure what I was touching but it wasn't good. It was no use, though. Without removing my head, there was no way I could reach the bottom. I looked at skinny little Timmy, but realized if my arms were too short, his arms definitely wouldn't reach. We stared at the can for a moment and then I got another brilliant idea.

"Timmy, come here," I motioned to the can. I used my hands to measure his head and then compared it with the opening on the garbage can. "Hmm."

"Fifth, what are you doing?" asked T-Bone. "You're not thinking what I think you're thinking, *are you?*"

"Well, it would fit," I said standing behind Timmy and pointing to his head and the garbage can.

"It's worth a shot," said T-Bone. "It could be 125 points."

"Exactly," said Tim. "Wait, what's worth a shot?"

"You'll see," I said. "Grab his feet."

I grabbed Timmy under the arms and T-Bone got his feet. We lifted him off of the ground and pointed his head toward the garbage can.

"Guys?" Timmy asked. "What are we doing?"

"Getting cups," I said matter-of-factly.

"But, guys…"

Before he could finish his sentence his head was already in the can. I looked around to see if anyone was watching and luckily, there weren't too many people hanging around.

"I got one!" hollered a voice from the can.

"Good, grab the sticker and get the rest," I instructed.

"It smells in here," Timmy moaned.

"It's a garbage can. What did you expect?" asked T-bone.

"Oh, yeah, right."

I wondered why I hadn't thought of it sooner. At this rate, I figured, we'd be able to buy a car for my parents and one for me. When he grabbed the last sticker, we pulled him out. He had a coffee stirrer stuck to his head and he smelled like a dump.

"Good job," T-Bone said, knocking the stirrer out of his hair and holding his nose.

"Yeah, good job," I told him, from a distance. "Let's keep going."

"More garbage cans?" Timmy asked.

"A few," I said, winking at T-Bone.

"Okay, just a few more," Timmy nodded.

By the time we were ready to leave, we had filled up four more books. I had no idea how many points we had earned, but it had to be a lot. We stood at the bus stop and within five minutes, Sandy pulled up.

"Hey, Sandy," said T-Bone.

"Hi boys, how was your day?"

"Good," T-Bone answered. "How was your route?"

"Okay," she said, covering her nose. "Were you boys playing at the dump?"

"Not quite," I answered, knocking a piece of lettuce off of Timmy's back.

Chapter Ten

All The Kids Are Wearing Them

On the third day, my alarm went off like a cannon. I felt like I was getting up to go to work and wondered how adults did it everyday. It looked easy enough, but if this was what working was like, I was glad I was a kid.

At eight o'clock, Timmy came into my room with a bandanna on his head and an air freshener around his neck.

"What's that?" I asked.

"My garbage can gear."

"Okay," I said, rolling my eyes.

"Hey, boys," my mom said, poking her head

into my room. "You're not going to the mall again, are you?"

"Actually, we are," I said.

"Well, I'd love to know what is so exciting at the mall and why Timmy's wearing an air freshener."

"It's the new thing," I said.

"The new thing?" my mom asked.

"Yeah, all the kids are wearing them."

"Then where's yours?" my mom asked kind of suspiciously.

"Right here," Timmy said, pulling an apple air freshener out of his pocket.

"Well, it looks weird, but I guess it can't hurt."

I pulled the air freshener over my head and smiled. At 9 o'clock we met T-Bone at the bus stop and waited.

"What's with the air fresheners?" asked T-Bone.

"They're the new thing," Timmy answered.

"No, they're not," I said, smacking the back of his head. "I said that to mom because she was suspicious."

"Oh, so they're not cool?" asked Timmy.

"Not unless you're a mini van," T-Bone laughed.

We walked into the mall and went right to our bench, at least our half of the bench. Uncle Sam was sitting there, as happy as usual. I sat on my half and T-Bone and Timmy went to check out the crowd at Wrangler Ray's.

"Good morning," I said.

"Morning," Uncle Sam mumbled. Wow, that's progress, I thought.

I don't know if it was curiosity or the fact that we would be spending the better part of a day on the same three foot bench, but I decided to find out why he was so miserable.

"So, do you come here everyday?" I asked.

"What are you writing a book?"

"No," I said.

"Yes," he grumbled. "I come here everyday. Does that answer your question?"

"My first one," I said sarcastically, "But why?"

"What do you mean why?"

"I mean, why do you sit here everyday? Doesn't your wife miss you?"

"No, my wife doesn't miss me," he grumbled.

"I miss her. She died two years ago. Satisfied?"

"Oh," I said, my stomach sinking. I never figured there could be a real reason he was so miserable. All this time I had been picturing him as a miserable baby, kid, and grown-up and now, this changed everything. Suddenly, I had nothing to say.

"Cat got your tongue?" he asked in a sad voice.

"What do you mean?"

"It means, just like everyone else, once you find out why I'm so grumpy, you've got nothing to say."

"I don't think you're mean," I lied.

"Sure you don't. You think I'm a peach. Don't you see the kids and birds that flock to me? Why, I'm as popular as Santa Claus."

"Well, you're definitely not the friendliest guy in the world, but I wouldn't call you mean."

"Since I lost my wife, I guess I've been mad at the world."

"Losing your wife really sucks," I said.

He looked over and smiled. "You know, kid, you're the first person to say it like it is. Everyone says time heals all wounds and I was lucky to have her as long as I did. You're the first person to just say it like it is and you're right, it really sucks."

"Whew," I said, "I was just about to apologize."

"Don't apologize, just do me a favor and take off that apple air freshener. It smells worse than your brother did yesterday."

"How do you know my brother stunk? We never even came back up here."

"I saw you boys from over the railing, shoving him into a garbage can and then I had the joy of smelling him on the bus."

"You were on the bus, too?"

"I was in the back and *we all smelled him*."

"I have another question, Sam," I continued, "what's your *real* name?"

"Sorry about that," he said with a guilty smile. "My name is George."

Just as I was making progress, Timmy appeared with stickers up and down his arms.

"Nicky, look!" Timmy shouted. "Look at this!"

"That's cool," I said. "Go get more."

"Alright," he said, running back to work.

"While we're answering questions, or at least I am, I have a question for you," said George. "Since we both know that you aren't collecting points for old people, what are you boys doing with all of these stickers?"

"We're collecting points to get my parents a 15th anniversary present," I explained. "My mom has been dropping a lot of hints."

George just smiled.

"What?" I asked, confused by his smile.

"That just reminds me of something my kids did for Martha and me for our anniversary."

I started laughing.

"What?" he asked.

"George and Martha? George and Martha? Did you know that George Washington was married to a woman named Martha?"

"Really? I had no idea. Let me congratulate you on being the first person to point that out. That's quite fascinating," he said, rolling his eyes.

"Oh," I said, realizing that it's not as funny if it's old news. "Well?"

"Well, what?" he asked.

"What did your kids do?"

"They ate 25 subs."

"You must have some big kids," I said.

"Not all at once," he said, rolling his eyes again. "They ate 25 subs so they could earn a free sub for our anniversary."

"Wow, that's all they gave you?"

"That's all?" he asked, rather insulted. "Those kids saved every penny to buy those 25 subs and they took the time to eat them all."

I couldn't help but think that my old friend Gino Pie could have done it in a week.

"So then," he continued, "on that night, they presented us with a sub, wrapped in a big bow. It was the best present we ever received."

"That was your best present?" I asked, wondering what the worst present could have been.

"Other than our kids, yes, that was the best present."

"Did you eat it?"

"No, I framed it. What do you think we did with it?"

"I just meant that I didn't know if you saved it because you liked it so much."

"Of course, I ate it," he said, staring at me like I was nuts. "The only thing better than the fact that they ate all of those sandwiches, was the look on their faces when we ate ours."

"You really liked it?"

"It was a great sub."

"No, I mean, you liked getting something so small for a present? Weren't you disappointed?"

"Listen, over the years, my kids have given us some very expensive, very nice presents and we appreciated them all, but that sub was the best. Coming in as a close second, though, would be the portrait."

"They drew you a picture?" I asked.

"No, they got dressed up and had a picture taken."

"What's the big deal about a picture?"

"The big deal," he started, "was that they did this by themselves and they did it for us. And trust me, getting those kids to have a picture taken was probably no easy task for my oldest."

"How did they do it," I asked, just in case the sticker idea didn't pan out and we needed a plan B.

"Not real sure," he said, "I just know my oldest son had his best friend take it and they had it developed and framed at the five and dime."

"The what?" I asked.

"The five and…never mind."

"Okay, new question," I warned. "If you have four kids, why are you here everyday? Are they afraid of you?"

"You know you're taking this honesty thing a little far," said George.

"Don't you want to see them?"

"The truth is, I used to see my kids all of the time."

"Then why not now?" I reminded him.

"Well, after my wife died I turned pretty sour and I didn't want to make them miserable. I decided to keep my distance."

"So, you just stopped talking to them?"

"No, we talk on the phone a lot, I just asked them to give me a little time."

"How much time?"

"You sound just like one of them," he smiled.

"Well, if Martha died two years ago, I'm sure they miss you. At least, I think they do. Then again, they don't know the new and grumpy you, do they?"

"That's why I stay away, kid. I don't want them to know the grumpy me."

"Did you ever think that if you spent time with them, you might not be so grumpy? I mean, I know how hard it would be to give up all of this" I said, pointing to the benches and the mall.

"Hey, look, someone threw out a cup downstairs," he said, obviously trying to end the conversation.

"Gotcha," I said. "I can take a hint."

"If you could take a hint, you wouldn't have come back the second day," he laughed.

Chapter Eleven

Sticker Shock

As the beginning of school drew closer, the deadline for collecting Wrangler Ray points was sneaking up on us. It was a rainy Tuesday when my mom announced that we would all be visiting the dentist.

"But we have to go to the mall!"

"Honey, you've been going to the mall every-day. I think you can skip a day."

"But we'll miss the lunch crowd," Timmy whined.

"The what?" my mom asked.

"He just likes the hustle and bustle of a busy mall," I said, giving Timmy a look.

There was no way around this one. My mom was a stickler for doctor and dentist appointments. When we got back, T-Bone was on the front steps.

"What's up?" I asked.

"Since we can't go to the mall, I think we should count our points."

We sat on the floor in my room and dumped all of the books out of T-Bone's box. There had to be a million points in those books and I couldn't wait to add them up and look in the catalog. Before we started I grabbed a calculator.

"You don't need that," said T-Bone, pointing to his head. "I can do it all up here."

"Fine, let's just get going," I said, slowly calling out sticker amounts. "Twenty-five, ten, twenty-five, fifteen, twenty-five, twenty-five..."

"Slow down," T-Bone hollered with his eyes closed. He may have been trying to add numbers in his head, but he looked like he pulled a muscle. "What do you think, I'm an adding machine?"

"I'm getting the calculator," I snapped.

We decided to add up the books and then add them again to make sure we did it right.

Unfortunately, we never came up with the same number twice. Finally, we decided to add each book separately and then add all of the books. When our grand total came out the same twice we stopped. I reached for the catalog book that listed the prizes. The book had been at T-Bone's house and this was my first chance to really look at our choices.

"Alright," I said, opening the cover, "we have 13,225 points. Where should we send my parents?"

"Somewhere hot," T-Bone nodded.

"Definitely," I agreed, opening the catalog.

The room suddenly went quiet. T-Bone was watching me as I stared at the catalog. I knew he was dense, but until this moment, I had no idea how dense.

"T-Bone," I asked quietly, "when you looked at the prizes, did you happen to notice how many points you needed?"

"What?" he asked.

"I said, when you looked at the prizes, did you happen to notice how many points you needed?"

"Not really. Why?" he asked innocently.

"Because" I said, gritting my teeth and taking

a deep breath with each word, "it seems that you need 100,000 points for a three-day trip and 500,000 points for a car that only seats two people."

"Yeah?"

"Do you also realize that we don't quite have 100,000 points and if we did have half a million points, what would my parents do with a two-seater?"

"Honestly Nick, if we got your dad the car, he'd moan about the insurance and if we sent them on a trip, he'd probably get a sunburn. So this is probably a blessing. Anyway, remember, the catalog is filled with valuable prizes, it says so right here. We'll just find them something else. No problem."

Suddenly, T-Bone sounded like my grandfather with his talk of blessings. Unfortunately, I wasn't in the mood and I threw the catalog at him.

"So why exactly did we spend everyday at the mall, shoving my brother into garbage cans?" I asked, noticing how stupid some of these valuable prizes really were. "Was it to get my parents matching Wrangler Ray sun visors?"

"Come on, you know you enjoyed shoving

Timmy in the garbage cans," T-Bone smirked. "And did you know the visors have a strap where you can hook your soda to a hanging straw and you can actually wear the soda right on your head?"

"Yeah, after all of this, I want to see my mom wear a Wrangler Ray soda on her head. Right now, I never want to see another Wrangler Ray soda for as long as I live."

"Alright, calm down," said T-Bone. "I have another idea. Why don't we make a list of all of the prizes we have enough points for?"

"That won't take long," I grumbled.

T-Bone grabbed some paper and I started reciting the prizes we could afford. Let's see, free sodas, free burgers, matching sippy visors, Wrangler Ray cowboy hats, key chains, bandannas, backpacks, can openers, alarm clocks. My heart began to sink. After embarrassing ourselves, harassing people, and picking through garbage cans the most I could give my parents was a backpack filled with a can opener and bandannas.

"Okay, then, see how many points we need for a decent prize," he suggested.

"Well, if we both quit school and spend the next twenty-seven years at the mall, we might be able to get them a television," I snapped.

"Let me see that catalog," he said.

"We're sunk," I moaned, plopping on my bed. "We haven't had one person call for an odd job, I have no gift for my parents, and I've wasted the last days of summer shoving Timmy into garbage cans!"

"Not so fast," said T-Bone. "Do your parents like coffee?"

"What?"

"You heard me. Do they like coffee?"

"I guess they like it. Don't all grown-ups?"

"Well," said T-Bone, "according to Wrangler Ray, if we had 16,000 points we could get them a coffee maker."

"T-Bone," I said tapping the numbers on my calculator, "we're like 2,775 points away."

"How many stickers is that?"

"One hundred eleven large sodas," I said, feeling even worse. I began wondering if we should have taken the easy route and just done a family picture. I decided to recount the money in my blue sock. Maybe there was a fifty dollar bill that I had missed. Unfortunately, there was no fifty dollar bill and because of bus fare, the sock was almost empty. The only things left were my valuables - my grandfather's baby ring, my first tooth, and pictures of me and my friends from Philadelphia. It looked like we'd need Plan B, the family portrait.

"Hey, T-Bone, how are you at taking pictures?" I asked.

"They don't call me Kodak for nothing."

"No one calls you Kodak," I reminded him.

"Well, they would if they saw my work."

"Your work?"

"Yes, my work," he repeated. "I'm quite handy behind the little glass window that you look through before you push the little button thing."

"You're also good with lingo, too," I said, rolling my eyes.

"Thanks, I work at it," T-Bone replied, another insult sailing right over his head.

"Well, I have an idea. Instead of giving my parents a coffee maker, let's use my mom's digital camera and get a picture of all of the kids, print it, and frame it."

"Why not give them both?" T-Bone suggested. "We can still get the rest of the stickers before school starts and how hard is it to take one picture?"

"Fine, whatever," I said, "but just to be on the safe side, can you take the picture?"

"How am I supposed to be in the picture and take the picture?" he protested.

"You're not going to be in the picture, moron."

"What do you mean?" he asked, forgetting, once again, that he wasn't one of my parents' actual children.

"I mean, it's supposed to be a picture of the four kids in my family," I explained.

"Okay," he said, quickly recovering. "I'll come over tomorrow morning and we can do it."

After he left, I snuck around, picking out clothes for the girls. It was harder than I thought, so I decided to just copy the outfits from the last Easter picture. I found their dresses, hats, and buckle shoes. I figured once we dressed them and Timmy and I put on our suits, that the whole thing would take a few minutes. The only other thing I needed to know was what a five and dime was.

Chapter Twelve

At Least A Thousand Words

When I woke up the next morning, I was exhausted. I knew T-Bone would be over soon and we weren't ready. Luckily, my mom told me she would be working out in the yard for a while. If she stayed outside long enough, I would be able to get everyone dressed and have the picture taken before she finished. For good reason, I still hadn't told Timmy or the girls what we were doing. I woke Timmy up first and naturally, he jumped out of bed.

"I know what I'll wear," he said running to his closet, pulling out a Philadelphia Flyers hockey jersey.

"No, no," I said, remembering what George's kids did. "You have to get dressed up."

"You mean wear the Flyers baseball hat, too?" he asked.

"No, like Sunday clothes or Christmas clothes," I explained.

His mouth dropped.

"Why can't I wear what I want?"

"Because you can't," I said, grabbing his suit and tie out of the closet.

"Oh, no you don't," he hollered. "I'd rather go back in the garbage can."

"That could be arranged," I sneered, even though I hated wearing suits as much as he did. "Now, get dressed so you can help me dress the girls."

As I entered the hallway, I could still hear him moaning and groaning and mumbling under his breath. Too bad, I thought. I opened Maggie's door and looked at her bed. There were so many rag dolls and stuffed animals on top that I wasn't even sure if she was there.

"Maggie, are you in here?" I asked, turning on the light. I inspected the bed and saw no sign of her anywhere. Finally, I noticed a foot. I grabbed it and pulled.

"Oww," cried a voice from underneath the covers.

"Maggie, get up. We have to take a picture."

"Take it where?" she whined.

"What?"

"You take it," she hollered.

"Maggie, wake up. T-Bone is taking a picture of us with a camera," I explained.

Her head popped up from the pile of dolls and with only one eye open, she asked why we were taking a picture. Not having time to explain, I ignored her. She repeated the question a dozen times and I continued to ignore her until she grabbed my ears and we were nose to nose.

"I said why are we taking a picture?"

"If I tell you, you have to promise not to tell mom or dad."

"Why? Are we gonna get arrested?"

"No, we're not gonna get arrested," I explained. "We're giving mom and dad a picture of us for their anniversary."

"Why?"

"Because a picture will make a nice gift."

"A picture will make a nice gift?" she asked suspiciously.

"Yeah, now get up," I demanded.

"Well, why do we have to give them another picture? They have lots and lots of picture books. Take one from there."

"We're not using an old picture from the photo albums. Just get up," I hollered, tired of repeating myself and tired of explaining why.

"Then I'm wearing my bathing suit," Maggie announced.

"Oh no, you're not."

"Oh, yes, I am!" she exclaimed.

Before I could answer her, I heard Timmy yelling. I ran down the hallway, caught a glimpse of something strange and backed up.

"What is that?" I asked.

Pausing between each word, he hollered, "My... good... clothes!"

"What are you talking about? These can't be your good clothes. You look like an elf."

"They're too small, Nick. I'm telling you

they're too small."

"Well, put something on that fits," I hollered.

"I don't have anything that fits. There's no fancy holidays in the summer."

"That's all you have?" I asked, glancing in his closet.

"Until mom takes us shopping again," he snapped. "Now, what am I supposed to do?"

"Just hold on," I told him, "let me think for a minute." I considered lending him some of my clothes but he was much smaller than I was and I figured he'd go from looking like an elf to looking like a hobo. I was in the middle of thinking when Emma came walking into Timmy's room.

"Hi," she said, unaware of the chaos.

"Look, Emma," I said kneeling down, "we're going to take a picture for mommy and daddy. It's going to be a surprise because it's a present for their anniversary and it will make them smile and be really happy."

"Okay," she answered.

Finally, I thought, someone ready to cooperate. No questions, no moaning, and no whining, just - okay.

"Now, can you go in your room and get the pretty dress hanging on the door knob?"

"Okay," she answered, just like a little angel.

"Alright, Timmy, you need something to wear. Do you have black pants?"

"That fit?" he asked.

"Of course, that fit," I hollered.

"Then no," he answered.

"Blue?" I asked.

"No."

"Brown?"

"No."

"Alright, hold on," I said, knowing that he had gotten taller and was probably telling the truth. "Let me see if I have anything too small for me."

I went through my closet and found a pair of black pants that might work. I also grabbed a vest. When I returned to Timmy's room, I could hear Maggie's famous tattling song.

"Ooooh, oooooh, I'm telling. Oooooh, oooooh, you're in trouble."

Two seconds later, Maggie entered Timmy's room, dragging Emma behind her. When Maggie finally let go and Emma raised her head, I was speechless. Naturally, Maggie wasn't.

"Look, Nicky. Look what Emma did and it's not gonna come off. Look, Nicky."

"Emma?" I gasped, "What were you thinking? Why did you do this? Are you trying to kill me?"

Emma had taken a green magic marker and drew glasses and a moustache on her face. Not only was I sure they wouldn't come off in time for the picture, I was pretty sure they would never come off.

"You said we had to make mom and dad smile and I wanted to make them laugh," she explained with a big smile.

And there you had it. I looked around the room and realized that a family portrait may not have been the way to go. Timmy was swimming in my dress pants, complimented with a Flyers jersey and a tie. Maggie was wearing a two piece bathing suit, flip flops, and sunglasses. Unfortunately, the two pieces didn't match and the flip flops were on the wrong feet. And Emma, little Emma, looked like an unshaven fly with her huge green glasses and moustache. There was no way we could take a picture now.

No sooner had I made the decision to cancel the picture when a camera flash went off and T-Bone burst through the door.

"What are you doing?" I hollered.

"You asked me to take pictures," he said, looking around. "What the heck is going on?"

"I'm trying to get everyone dressed."

"Dressed as what?" he laughed.

"The picture is now officially off!" I exclaimed.

"Why?" he asked.

"Oh, I don't know, because my brother and sisters aren't exactly *fancy*."

"That's the beauty of it," said T-Bone. "My mom is always framing the funny pictures. She says they're the ones that really tell a story."

"Are you nuts? Exactly what kind of a story would we be telling? Mom and dad, here is a picture of your four dopey kids."

"I'm telling you, it's pretty funny," T-Bone said, trying to hold back the laughter. "you look like circus clowns and that's funny! Let me take a few pictures."

"No," I insisted.

"Come on, your parents will love it."

"No," I repeated, "this is not how the picture should look."

Before we could finish arguing, he had taken another picture. When the kids saw the flash again, they ran next to me, smiled, and yelled, "Cheese."

"Good, good, good," said T-Bone as he lined up each picture. I didn't have a good feeling about this at all, but I hoped that T-Bone was right. Maybe one of these pictures could be a keeper. Maybe it would be something we would laugh about for years. I doubted it, but I was desperate.

When the big photo shoot was over, mismatched bathing suit, green glasses and all, we checked out our work. Each picture was more ridiculous than the one before. As we flipped through them, I realized they were funny and printed some. I still wasn't sure what a five and dime was, but since it was a digital camera, I figured we didn't need one. Since I used all of my money on bus fare, I decided to find a frame in our house. There was a picture of Emma and Maggie at the beach in a big frame so I grabbed it, took out their picture and replaced it with the new one. Then I attempted to scrub Emma's face. Luckily, she used a washable marker and by the time I was done her skin was red, but there was no sign of the glasses or the moustache.

What would my parents think? I wondered if we should have just given them a sub. But my mom taught Kindergarten and she was used to finding the best in the most ridiculous projects. She's been framing our lousy artwork for years so I figured T-Bone's work might actually fit right in.

Chapter Thirteen

Hiccup Drive

The next morning was raining, a typical muggy New Jersey day. Since we had decided to give my parents the picture and the coffee maker, we went back to the mall. While it wasn't a trip to the Bahamas, compared to the matching Wrangler Ray sippy visors, the coffee maker would be an improvement. Luckily, Sandy pulled up before we floated away.

"Good morning boys," she said with her usual chipper attitude.

"Hey," I nodded.

"Good morning," T-Bone and Timmy chirped together.

"How's the cup business treating you?"

"Not good," I mumbled.

"How come?" she asked.

"Because someone didn't read the prize cata-log and now we don't even have enough points for a coffee maker."

Sandy raised her eyebrow and looked at T-Bone. "Well, maybe this will help," she said pulling out Wrangler Ray sticker point books.

"What's this?" T-Bone asked.

"My contribution," she said with a wink.

We opened the book. It was full of stickers.

"I don't get it," I said.

"Well, a lot of my riders bring their cups on the bus so I started asking them to put their stickers in the book. There's 1,000 points from me and 1,000 points from George."

"George?" I asked. "As in George and Martha? George?"

"The one and only," she winked.

"Now, I really don't get it."

"George put the word out on the benches and the seniors started collecting stickers. It's the first time in years that I've seen him excited about something. It's kind of nice."

"But why?"

"He likes you," she smiled.

"How can you tell?"

"Don't let him fool you. He's really an old softy. He also wanted me to give you this," she said handing me an envelope.

Still confused, I stuck the envelope in my pocket and tried to calculate how many stickers we would need. When we arrived at the mall, we went straight to our bench and there was no sign of George. I figured he was in the rest room. T-Bone and Timmy got started and I scanned the other benches. For the first time, I took a good look at the people on the benches. I wondered how they ended up here everyday. Until George, I never even noticed them. Since George, I realized that they each have a story. Most of them probably have families and like George, probably some sadness.

"Nick, Nick, look at this, 200 points," said Timmy.

"Good job!" I said, giving him a high five.

As Timmy walked back to Wrangler Rays I wondered what would happen to us when we grew up. Could one of us end up alone on a mall bench or would we be happy like our grandfather? As I pondered the mysteries of life, I realized George had still not returned to the bench and remembered the envelope in my pocket. I pulled it out and carefully unfolded it. I wasn't sure what to expect, but it looked like a letter.

Dear Nicky,

You're probably too young to understand, but I want to thank you. You reminded me that I do have a family. I'm staying at my son's this week, so I won't be seeing you before school starts. Please accept the points we've collected. Everyone pitched in and we hope we've helped you get something special. Just remember, special doesn't mean big and fancy, it could be as simple as a sub or a picture.

Your friend,
George

P.S. Sandy gave me your flyer and I'd like to hire you and your friend to rake my leaves and straighten out my garage. Stop by after school one day. The address is 234 Hiccup Drive.

Wow, I thought, George lives on a street with a goofier name than mine. Then a small piece of paper dropped out. I turned it over and it was a copy of a black and white picture of four goofy kids. One was wearing pajamas, one was wearing a cowboy outfit, one was wearing a dress, and the oldest one was dressed up and looking frustrated.

"What's that?" asked T-Bone, his arms covered with stickers.

"It's a letter from George."

"Who?"

"George, dopey, the old guy who sits here everyday."

"Oh, you mean old crabby."

"No, the guy that gave us 1,000 points and just hired us to rake his yard and clean his garage."

"Sweet old guy," T-Bone smiled.

"What's with the picture?"

"It's nothing," I said, placing the letter and picture back in the envelope.

"T-Bone, T-Bone, a whole bunch of people just walked in," exclaimed Timmy, peeling off a dozen stickers and returning to work.

And with that, the morning took a turn for the better. We were close to getting a coffee maker, the goofy picture seemed better, and we got our first odd job. I even felt good about George visiting his son. If it wasn't for me, I thought, he'd still be sitting on the bench.

"What's with you?" asked T-Bone.

"Huh?"

"What's with the big goofy smile on your face."

"I was thinking, that if it wasn't for me, George may not have gotten back with his kids," I said proudly. "He might have spent the rest of his life on this bench. I wonder what I said to make such a big difference."

"Maybe it wasn't what you said," T-Bone explained.

"What do you mean?"

"Maybe he just wanted to get away from you," T-Bone laughed.

It took until 2 o'clock, but we did it. We collected enough points for a coffee maker and even had enough left over for four sodas and four cheeseburgers. We celebrated.

When Sandy picked us up, I couldn't wait to ask her more questions.

"Hi boys," she smiled. "What's the word?"

"The word is good. We collected enough points for a coffee maker and lunch," I said, handing her a bag containing the fourth cheeseburger and soda."

"What's this?" she asked.

"Just a little thank you. By the way, did you know that George hired us for some odd jobs?"

"Actually," she started, "you'll probably be getting a lot of calls. George passed them out in his neighborhood."

"Really?" I asked. "Where is his neighborhood?"

"The other end of your neighborhood," she laughed.

When we got off of the bus, we thanked Sandy again. With school starting soon we probably wouldn't see her for a while. She said it was a pleasure to know us and I think she meant it. T-Bone came over and we filled out the order form for the coffee maker. I placed George's letter with all of my other valuables, in the blue sock in my sock drawer.

Chapter Fourteen

If These Plants Could Talk

No matter how hard I tried to make time slow down, the last week of the summer seemed to fly by. If only I could find a way to make time fly that fast during math class. Before I knew it, I was waking up at six and back on the bus. While I dreaded the end of summer, going back to school wasn't as bad as I imagined. It was good to see some of my old friends and T-Bone and I turned out to be semi-celebrities. Our teachers congratulated us on becoming unofficial Junior Ambassadors for New Jersey. On the second day of school, our principal asked us to write a column about our upcoming Garden State Adventures for the school newspaper.

Before we agreed, I contacted the Governor's Office to see if they still wanted us. I was relieved when they said, "Yes." I think we were both worried that they would have forgotten all about us. Besides working for New Jersey, we also started getting calls for odd jobs. Most of the jobs were pretty normal, but some were definitely odd.

One old lady asked us to come over twice a week and water her plants. It sounded like a normal job until we found out that she had seventy-four plants and she wanted us to talk to each one of them. We thought that was weird until, pretending to be the plants, *she spoke back to us.* Poor T-Bone spent two weeks believing she had magical plants. He was even planning on asking her if he could borrow them for the science fair.

Another lady, who lived on the other end of town, in an enormous house with her own maid, asked us to cut coupons from the Sunday paper because she had arthritis. Since I had spent many hours cutting coupons for my dad, I figured it would be easy. And, it wouldn't have been bad, except that she bought about eighteen newspapers every Sunday and she wanted every single coupon cut out and cut out neatly. She didn't have a pet but we had to cut out coupons for dog and cat food. She didn't have a car but she wanted the coupons for motor oil and car wax. One day, I spotted all of the coupons from the week before in the garbage can. I found her housekeeper, Gloria, and wondering if it was an accident, asked her if she knew that the coupons were in the garbage.

"Look around here," she said, as she scrubbed a pot. *Unlike T-Bone, she had a real Jamaican accent.*

"Yeah?"

"Don't ever say that I told you, but Mrs. Muncie really doesn't need to cut out coupons."

"Then why did she hire us?" I asked.

"She believes in rewarding initiative."

"In what?" I asked.

"You boys could be hanging out on the streets,causing trouble, but instead you chose to earn money the old fashioned way…that's initiative."

"Oh," I said, sounding a little disappointed

that we had a fake job.

"Don't be upset," she smiled, "it makes her happy and it is teaching you the value of a dollar and hard work."

"But why does she make us neatly cut out every single coupon if she's only throwing them out?" I wondered.

"Mrs. Muncie believes in an honest day's pay for an honest day's work. She wants you to earn every penny just like Mr. Muncie did."

"He must have been really rich," I observed.

"Let's just say that he was very, very comfortable," she winked.

"Did he start out working as a kid?"

"He started at eleven years old, selling newspapers during the Great Depression and then moved onto other odd jobs; whatever he could find. He was a hard worker and it paid off."

"Do you think I'll be comfortable one day?"

"I think that's what Mrs. Muncie wants you to see and that's why, even though you know the truth, you must continue to come."

"Even though I know she's just throwing

them away?"

"Absolutely."

With that I decided to keep Gloria's secret and not to tell T-Bone about Mrs. Muncie. Knowing T-Bone, he'd offer to fold the dirty clothes before they went into the wash.

Some of our jobs were pretty straight forward, like mowing lawns or cleaning garages. A couple of people asked us to walk their dogs and one lady tried to talk us into babysitting her four year old son while she worked in her office. We declined. George hired us often and recommended us to everyone. It was hard to believe that he was the same man we first met on the bench. I wondered if we would have had any jobs *if we had picked a different bench.*

We decided we liked working for old ladies better than anyone because they not only paid us; they fed us. They usually gave us cookies, cake, or pie. I was glad Gino Pie still lived in Philly because he would have worked just for the food and put us out of business. I had to hand it to my mom, though. Her odd job idea was pretty smart and my blue sock was almost filled. Pretty soon, I'd have to expand to a two-sock operation.

Chapter Fifteen

Valuable Prizes Indeed

It was the second week of September and I had just returned from a job when the doorbell rang. I stopped to count how many rings, in case it was one of my sisters. When it only rang once, I ran to the front door. It was a delivery man holding a big cardboard box.

"Is Nick Abruzzi home?" he asked.

"That's me," I said.

"This is probably for your father, kid," the delivery man said, without looking up.

"No, I'm pretty sure it's for me."

"How do you know it isn't for your father?" he asked.

"Well," I paused, "for one thing, my father's name is Jim."

"Oh," said the delivery man, "sign here."

"No problem," I replied, "this must be my coffee maker."

"Your what?" he asked, very confused.

"My coffee maker," I said proudly.

"Coffee can stunt your growth, kid."

"I'll make a note of it," I said, grabbing the box.

I called T-Bone and he ran right over. We stared at the box for about ten minutes. We weren't sure if we should open it, but we wanted to take a peek.

"C'mon, let's open it," urged T-Bone.

"I don't know," I warned, "what if we can't get it back into the box?"

"Good point," he agreed. "My dad says the boxes shrink a after you take everything out."

"Yeah, sure, the boxes shrink," I laughed.

"Seriously," he insisted. "Did you ever try to get something back in the box?"

"Alright," I said, just as anxious as T-Bone was to tear into the box. "Just pay attention to how it's packed so we can get it back in."

Once we started, I knew there was no way we could get everything back into the box. I held the Styrofoam while T-Bone gently pulled the box. There was no turning back. We carefully removed each piece, starting with the glass pot, the filter basket, and the machine. When it was all out, we stared at it.

"Pretty cool, huh?" asked T-Bone.

"Yeah," I said.

We stared a little longer, like we were waiting for it to do something. I had been expecting this package for two weeks and somehow it wasn't as exciting as I thought it would be. Maybe it was because I didn't like coffee. Maybe it was because I had no interest in appliances. Whatever the reason, I hoped my parents were more excited.

"Do your parents even like coffee?" T-Bone wondered.

"I guess," I answered, never considering the fact that there might be a reason they didn't have a coffee maker. "Don't all grown ups like coffee?"

"When are you gonna give it to them?"

"Well, their anniversary is tomorrow, so I

guess tomorrow. But I don't know how we're going to be able get it back into the box?"

"Maybe you don't have to," he suggested.

"What do you mean?"

"Well, you could set it up and put a ribbon on it."

"Not bad," I nodded, "not bad."

"Hide it in your room and we'll bring it out tomorrow."

"We'll?" I asked.

"You don't think I'm gonna miss the big moment, do you?"

"I guess not," I answered, "just don't get on his nerves. It's his anniversary, too, you know."

"Who? Me?" he laughed.

That night I had Timmy and the girls make a card and we all signed our names, even T-Bone. I found a big red bow in my mom's wrapping paper bin and placed it on top of the coffee maker. I also found a gift bag for the fancy family portrait.

When I came home from school the next day, I asked my mom if T-Bone could eat over.

"Sure," she said. "Does he like pork chops?"

"I think he likes anything at 5 o'clock," I

laughed.

"Then that's when we'll eat," she announced.

Dinner started right at five and my dad just shook his head when he saw T-Bone at the table. When dinner was over, I asked my parents not to get up.

"What's going on?" asked my mom.

"We have a surprise for you," I said. "Close your eyes."

"You want me to close my eyes with Tommy here?" asked my dad.

"Jim, just do what the kids want," my mom insisted.

"Alright, but you break it you bought it," he told T-Bone.

While they closed their eyes, we brought out the coffee maker, the card, and the gift bag with the portrait. We set them up on the counter and took a deep breath.

"Okay, you can open your eyes," I announced.

"Happy Anniversary," everyone shouted.

"Mommy, wait until you see what Emma

did," Maggie tattled.

"No tattling, Maggie," said my mom. "Now, where is this surprise?"

"Right here," I said, sliding to one side.

"Oh, my goodness," my mom shrieked. "You remembered our anniversary and got us gifts!"

"How could we forget? You left us enough hints!" I laughed.

"What hints?" my mom blushed.

"The little hints," I said, "like spelling 15th Anniversary on the fridge in magnets."

"You thought those hints were for you?" she laughed.

"Then who were they for?" I asked, more confused than ever. "You and dad already know about it, so it had to be for me."

We both turned and looked at my dad who was staring at the floor. The bad news was that he had forgotten another occasion. The good news, for him, was that my mom was so excited, she didn't even mind.

"Look at the card first," said Maggie. "Me and Emma drewed it and everybody in our family is in it, even T-Bone."

"Well, it's the most beautiful card I've ever seen," my mom said, hugging the girls.

"It's great, girls," said my dad, grabbing them both and kissing their foreheads.

"That's not all," said Timmy, pointing to the coffee maker. "Is anyone thirsty?"

"Is that for us?" my mom gasped.

"Yeah, and you'll never guess how we got it," exclaimed Timmy.

"That's not important," I said, nudging him in the back. "Do you like it?"

"We love it!" said my mom. "But how could you kids afford such a nice coffee maker? This had to be really expensive."

"And valuable," T-Bone added.

"Tommy probably won it," my dad laughed.

"Not exactly, Mr. A.," said T-Bone, "but you're close."

While my mom examined the coffee maker, we were pretty proud of ourselves.

"You know our old coffee maker was so beat up, that when we moved, I threw it away and we never got around to replacing it."

"That's good, because I couldn't remember if we ever had one or if you like coffee," I admitted.

"That's really a great gift, guys," my dad said, even proud of T-Bone.

"The picture, the picture," Emma shouted, pointing to the gift bag.

"There's more?" asked my mom. "Well, this is the best anniversary ever!"

"Okay," I warned, "but you might hate this."

"We could never hate anything you give us," my mom gushed.

"I told you they'd have to like it," T-Bone whispered.

My parents sat down next to each other and slowly pulled the frame out of the bag. They stared at the picture and didn't say a word. We were convinced that they thought it was stupid. Then suddenly, we heard a peep, followed by another peep. We all looked around the room until we realized that the peeps were coming from my mom. When she raised her head, her eyes were all puffy and she was peeping even faster.

"This is the most amazing picture I have ever seen," she cried. "You have no idea how much I love this picture."

At first, it was weird. My dad didn't say anything but he had the same smile George had when he talked about the subs.

"I took that picture, Mrs. A.," said T-Bone proudly. "I think it may be my best work."

"I think you might be right," my mom said, hugging him. "I think you might be right."

My mom set the picture on the table and T-Bone was right. It was his best work. It was a keeper. My dad hugged me and Timmy and then hugged T-Bone. That's when we knew he really loved it.

"Well, I don't know what to say," my mom began, "except you kids are amazing and we can't thank you enough. All five of you did a great job and we're very proud. I don't know how you did it, but I'm sure glad you did!"

"Emma wrote on her face," Maggie tattled.

"Did not," yelled Emma.

"You did, too! You can see it in the picture," Maggie insisted.

"Now," said my mom, "that's not important."

"It isn't?" asked Timmy.

"No, it isn't," my mom smiled. "Nothing could ruin today."

"Good, because I think I spelled a lot of words wrong on my test today."

"Do they take off for spelling mistakes?" asked my dad.

"On a spelling test they do," Timmy mumbled with his head down.

My dad just rolled his eyes, but nothing could rain on my mom's parade. "That's okay, we'll talk about that later," she said, still smiling.

Wow, I thought, my mom took the bad news about Timmy's spelling test pretty good. I almost wished I had some bad news.

"So how did you get the coffee maker?" my dad asked, pulling T-Bone and I aside. "You didn't steal it, did you?"

"No, I didn't steal it," I answered, rather insulted. "Do you really think I would steal a coffee maker?"

"Yeah," said T-Bone, trying to help me out, "if we were gonna steal something, we'd have stolen

140

something cooler than a coffee maker."

My dad and I just stopped and looked at him.

"Not that we'd ever steal anything, Mr. A., I just meant that if we, like had to…never mind."

Luckily, my father knew that T-Bone wasn't the kind of kid to go around stealing things. If he had to describe him, he might say things like annoying, frustrating, or aggravating, but never thief.

My mom decided to try out the coffee maker and make a fresh pot of coffee. I took a good look at the picture and it did tell a story. I wasn't exactly sure what that story was, but it was definitely a story. When the coffee finished brewing, my mom and dad raised their coffee cups and toasted their anniversary while we clapped and cheered.

"You know, this is what it's all about," said my dad. "So, for all of your hard work, mom and I will be taking you all out tomorrow, even Tommy."

"That's a great idea," my mom agreed.

"Where?" Timmy yelled.

"I don't know," my dad laughed, "maybe another Garden State Adventure! I'll let you know tomorrow."

Since we didn't know what the exact plans were, T-Bone called his mom to see if he could sleep over. As usual, his mom was more than happy to lend him out and we ran to his house to get a change of clothes. The next morning, my dad still wouldn't tell us what the plan was but I brought a notebook and camera just in case it was an adventure.

At 10:30, we piled into the van and much to my surprise, ended up at the mall. It was damp and chilly so I knew we wouldn't be doing anything outside.

"Hey, dad, do you know this is the mall?" I asked as we entered the parking lot.

"Of course, I know it's the mall," he answered.

"But you hate the mall," I reminded him. "Remember when you said you would rather be dipped in honey and left on an ant hill than go to the mall?"

"That's when we're shopping, but today we're not shopping," he assured us.

"Then what are we doing, dear?" asked my mom, as confused as the rest of us.

"Alright, if you must know, we're going to see a movie and then we're going bowling."

"But that's not a Garden State Adventure," I said, somewhat disappointed.

"Actually, since you boys are working for the Governor, I'm going to leave planning the adventures to you. Today is just family day."

"Good idea, Mr. A," said T-Bone. "I have a map and I made a list of places you can bring us."

"Fantastic," my dad sighed.

"Dad, do you know that the mall doesn't have a movie theater or a bowling alley?" I asked, now an expert of what the mall does have.

"Of course," he replied.

"Then why are we here?" I asked.

"You'll see," he said as he parked the van.

We got out of the car, put the girls in their strollers and walked through the main entrance. After spending so many days here with T-Bone and Timmy, it was weird walking around with my family. I was still checking for Wrangler Ray soda cups. Before I knew it, we stopped walking.

"Surprise," said my dad as we stood at the entrance to Wrangler Ray's. "I thought we'd have lunch at Wrangler Ray's today. You kids always ask us to eat here and we always say no, so I thought I'd surprise you."

T-Bone, Timmy, and I just looked at each other. We were definitely surprised. I looked at our bench and there were strangers sitting on it. Good, I thought, maybe George was with his family.

"And look at this," my dad continued. "I have buy-one-get-one-free coupons!"

Of course, he had coupons. We rarely ever ate or shopped anywhere that he didn't. We ordered our food and sat at the big tables in the middle. I realized that in the whole time we collected points, we only ordered food once, on the day that we got the last sticker. It was nice to eat inside, like normal people, without watching every person who was about to leave. I was happy we got the coffee maker, but I was happier to stop begging.

"Hey, look at this," said my dad, reading the back of his cup, "if you peel the little sticker off of your soda, you can earn prizes."

"No, Mr. A," corrected T-Bone, "you can win *valuable prizes!*"

Welcome to the Franklin Mason Press Guest Young Author Section

Turn this page for stories from our three newest Guest Young Authors, ages 9-12 years old. From thousands of submissions, these stories were selected by a committee for their creativity, originality, and quality.

Franklin Mason Press believes that children should have a paramount role in literature, including publishing and sharing their stories with the world. We hope you enjoy reading them as much as we did. If you would like to submit a story you have written, keep reading after the stories. Enjoy!

1st Place Guest Young Author

Zaneta Zachwieja
Age 10
Christopher Columbus School #8
Garfield, New Jersey

The Brave Mermaid

Splash! Splash! Isabel was soaking wet and then swam off. She was a beautiful mermaid and when she came home, here friends were waiting for her.

"Why were you on the surface?" they asked. I was picking flowers and Ig the Monster followed me, so I swam away.

She went to the playground with her friends and then everyone went home, When Isabel was almost at her house, Ig ran after her. She swam and swam until she found a sunken ship and hid inside. Then she found a net and trapped Ig.

When she came home, she told her parents,

but they couldn't think of anything to do, so after school she visited the smartest wizard. The wizard said, "I'll make a potion, but you'll have to come back after school tomorrow."

After school the next day, she went back to the wizard to get the potion and thanked him. The next day was the last day of school and Isabel packed her bags to make Ig good. She said goodbye to her family and began her journey. She had to travel 16 miles to get to Shark's Cove where Ig lived alone. Soon, she came to a dark forest, but she had to be careful because there were thorns on the trees and it was very dark. Then, she came to a stop at the deep canyon, hoping there was an entrance to the other side. But she came back to the top because there was no entrance. It was a dead end. She called her turtle friends and held onto their backs as they gave the tired mermaid a ride. Finally, she reached Ig's house, but had to rest.

The next day, Isabel woke up and found herself outside Ig's house. Luckily he was gone, so she went inside and poured the secret potion on his breakfast.

Later, Ig came home and ate his breakfast, but nothing happened. Isabel thought the potion was a failure, but then his eyes turned from red to blue and his frown turned into a smile. Back in her town, the Governor congratulated her for her success. Isabel got medals and so did Ig! During her speech, she said, "You should give the wizard a medal, too." So the Governor even gave a medal to the wizard. And, because he turned good, he no longer lived alone and went back to live with his family! Of course, he still remembered to visit Isabel's family, too!

2nd Place Guest Young Author

John Pascual
Age 11
Darby Elementary School
US Navy Base, Sasebo, Japan

The Easter Bunny Who Went Christmas

One Easter, the Easter Bunny was planning a special gift for all of the kids. He was really excited because every year the kids had Easter clothes, hats, and other accessories. Easter was every kids' favorite holiday. But when the Easter Bunny saw the kids this year, he was shocked.

He saw the kids with Christmas clothes, hats, and accessories! The Easter Bunny was incredibly sad. He went back to his house to think of a plan that would make him be noticed. Finally, he thought of something that would really work. He put all of his Easter clothes away, bought a Christmas costume, and changed his name to the Christmas Bunny.

Every Christmas, he would give eggs to the kids. If they were bad, they got coal in their eggs. If they were good, they would get a small toy in it...not what they wanted for Christmas. When the kids saw the Christmas Bunny, they complained to him.

"What happened to Easter? Why did you change your name to the Christmas Bunny?" asked the kids.

"Because I saw you kids wearing Christmas things and not Easter things," said the Bunny in a sad voice.

"We're sorry," said the kids. "Are you going to change your name back and host Easter again?"

The Bunny thought about it, and then said, "Yes, I will." The kids were all happy.

One year later, when it was Easter again, the kids ran up to the Easter Bunny's door and screamed, "Happy Easter!"

"Thank you for this," said the happy Bunny.

Then, from that day on, Easter was the way it should be and the Easter Bunny never changed his name again!

3rd Place Guest Young Author
Sunnie Vitale
Age 10
Dr. Joyanne D. Miller Elementary School
Egg Harbor Township, New Jersey

<u>Bobby Christmas</u>

Once there was a ten year old boy named Bobby Christmas. Bobby lived in a town called "Orange Blossom." He went to school every morning, except weekends. His school was called The Best School Ever, but he didn't think it was the best school ever because everyone made fun of his last name. One boy, Ray, used to be Bobby's best friend until everyone made fun of him for hanging out with a kid named Christmas. So, Ray found some new friends and started making fun of Bobby, too, just to be cool. Now, Bobby despised him.

One Wednesday morning, Bobby met a ten year old boy named Jarred Salami. Everyone would make fun of him. But once he found Bobby Christmas, they started talking and soon became friends. They were friends for two whole months when kids started making fun of them for it. The next year, the kids met a girl named Carla Ham. She became the new, funny-last-name kid. She met the boys and they became friends, too.

Year after year, people would find new funny-last-name kids to tease and Bobby Christmas and his friends would always become friends with them. Now, Bobby is treated equally by the other students, *or at least the ones with funny-last-names!*

Calling all young authors...

Would you like to be a Guest Young Author?

If you are 9-12 years old and would like to be Franklin Mason Press's next Guest Young Author, read the directions, write your story, and send it in! The first, second, and third place winners receive $50.00, $40.00, and $30.00, respectively, a book, an award, and a party where you get to autograph books. Send us a 150-350 word story about something strange, funny or unusual. Your story may be fiction or non-fiction.

Turn the page for more details!

Contest Rules

1. Stories must be typed or written very neatly.

2. Stories containing any violence or inappropriate content will not be considered.

3. Name, age, address, phone number, school, and parent's signature must be on the back of all submissions.

4. All work must be original and completed solely by the child.

5. Franklin Mason Press reserves the right edit and/or print the submitted material. All work becomes property of Franklin Mason Press and will not be returned. Any work selected will is considered a work-for-hire and Franklin Mason Press reserves all rights.

6. There is no deadline for submissions. All submissions are considered for the most current title.

7. Only winners will be notified. Winners will also be listed on www.franklinmasonpress.com.

Send all submissions to:
> Franklin Mason Press
> Youth Submissions Editor
> PO Box 3808
> Trenton, NJ 08629

Helpful Hints

Write about what you know or what you enjoy.

Read your story out loud and **LISTEN** to it!

Create original characters rather than writing about your favorite cartoon.

Keep an idea notebook and whenever you get a great idea that you don't have time to write about, jot it down.

When looking for spelling mistakes, don't trust your eyes or computers, read each line backwards, like the editors do!

After you submit your story, don't wait by the mailbox, start your next story.

And, of course, enjoy writing!

About the Author, Lisa Funari Willever

Lisa Funari Willever wanted to be an author since she was in the third grade and often says if there was a Guest Young Author contest when she was a child, she would have submitted a story a day. *Maybe two a day on weekends!*

She has been a wedding-dress-seller, a file clerk, a sock counter *(really)*, a hostess, waitress, teacher, and author. While she loved teaching in Trenton, New Jersey, becoming an author has been one of the most exciting adventures of her life. She is a full-time mom and a *night-time author* who travels all over the world visiting schools. She has been to hundreds of schools in dozens of states, including California, South Dakota, Iowa, South Carolina, North Carolina, Florida, Delaware, Connecticut, New York, Pennsylvania, West Virginia, Ohio, Nevada, Idaho, Utah, Alabama, Louisiana, and even Sasebo, Japan.

Lisa has written several books for children and even a book for new teachers. Her critically acclaimed *Chumpkin* was selected as a favorite by First Lady Laura Bush and displayed at the White House, *Everybody Moos At Cows* was featured on the Rosie O'Donnell Show, and *Garden State Adventure* and *32 Dandelion Court* have been on the prestigious New Jersey Battle of the Books List. Her other titles include *You Can't Walk A Fish, The Easter Chicken, Maximilian The Great, Where Do Snowmen Go?, The Culprit Was A Fly, Miracle on Theodore's Street, Exciting Writing,* and *On Your Mark, Get Set, Teach. Nicky Fifth For Hire* is her thirteenth book and she is currently working on three new titles!

Lisa is married to Todd Willever, a Captain in the Trenton Fire Department. They have three children, Jessica, 8 years old, Patrick, 7 years old, and Timothy Todd, 1 year old. They are also preparing to adopt a little girl from Guatemala (*details in the next book!*)

Lisa was a lifelong resident of Trenton and while she is proud to now reside in the beautiful Mansfield Township, she treasures her 34 years in the city. She is a graduate of Trenton State College and loves nothing more than traveling with her family.

About the
Sunshine Foundation

Franklin Mason Press is very proud to donate a portion of each book sale to different children's charities. Like our picture book, Where Do Snowmen Go and the first two Nicky Fifth books, 32 Dandelion Court and Garden State Adventure, Nicky Fifth For Hire will benefit The Sunshine Foundation.

In case you aren't familiar with this magnificent and giving group of people, we'd love to tell you about them! The Sunshine Foundation was started by Philadelphia police officer, William Sample who grew to care about many of the patients he protected at St. Christopher's Hospital in Philadelphia. He wished he could grant their wishes and over 20 years later, he and the foundation have granted over 26,500 wishes for children 3 to 21 with diseases and disabilities. They even have a Dream Village in Florida! If you would like to know more, or even better, help them out, you can find them at:

www.sunshinefoundation.org

Nicky Fifth's
Newest Adventure

Nicky Fifth's popularity, both in and out of the state of New Jersey, has been overwhelming! We receive e-mails from families telling us that they are taking their families on Nicky's Garden State day trips!

As a result of the demand and author Lisa Funari Willever's love for the great Garden State, Nicky's newest adventure is called:

Nicky Fifth's Passport to the Garden State!

Follow Nicky and T-Bone as they become New Jersey's Unofficial Junior Ambassadors. This book includes a passport that may be stamped at various destinations throughout the state, an interactive website, and a scavenger hunt.

Visit www.franklinmasonpress.com for more details.

Do you have ideas for Nicky's adventures?

Do you know about a great place in New Jersey that not too many other people know about?

Send us an e-mail and tell us all about it! Maybe your idea will end up in the next Nicky Fifth book!

Visit www.franklinmasonpress.com